PUMPKIN SPICE & ORC'S DELIGHT

EVERSHIFT HAVEN #1

Aurelia Skye

Pumpkin Spice and Orc's Delight

Evershift Haven, Volume 1

Aurelia Skye

Published by Amourisa Press, 2024.

Blurb

I'M JUST A STRESSED-out attorney in a pink Volkswagen, stranded in a magical town I didn't believe could exist—and falling hard for my orc mechanic, who's all muscle, zero bodysuit.

I'm on my way from Chicago to Seattle for a legal conference, having decided to drive myself because I need more fun in my life, according to my sister, when I pass through a strange, shimmering barrier. My pink Volkswagen dies right after, and I have to walk to the closest town—Evershift Haven. I'm stunned to see how all-out these folks go for Halloween to appeal to the tourists. I'm even more surprised by just how hot the orc mechanic promising to fix my car within a week is, but I imagine he's a pasty geek under all that makeup and muscled bodysuit. Right?

About that. Evershift Haven isn't some gimmicky tourist town. Turns out, magic is real, and when their resident witch gets distracted, the barrier between their world and ours sometimes drops long enough for a lonely attorney who hates her job to slip through and discover magic awaits. And Throk isn't some pasty geek. All those green muscles and drool-worthy body belong to him, my orc mechanic.

I'm stuck in a place I never imagined could exist and having the time of my life. When it's time to go back to the real world? I don't want to think about that right now...

This is the first book in a series about a magical town that shifts itself to celebrate seasons, holidays, and whatever random thing takes its fancy. It's lighthearted, humorous, and meant to make you feel as cozy as wearing a sweater while sipping pumpkin spice latte. The story is sweet, but there's definitely a pinch of sexy.

Chapter 1

I GRIP THE STEERING wheel tighter as my car speeds down the endless stretch of highway. The monotonous landscape blurs past my window, a sea of green and brown punctuated by the occasional billboard or gas station. My gaze flicks to the GPS on my dashboard, its robotic voice guiding me toward Seattle.

"Why did I think driving was a good idea, Suzette?" I ask myself, shifting in the seat of my bright pink Volkswagen Bug, complete with lady eyelashes on the eyes—a gift from my sister, Candice. The leather creaks beneath me, reminding me how long I've been sitting. My tailbone aches, and I roll my shoulders, trying to work out the stiffness.

As I pass another mile marker, I remember why I thought I'd take a mini-vacay. It's been over a year since I've taken any real time off. When was the last time I did something just for me, not for the firm or my clients?

I shake my head, refocusing on the road. The legal conference in Seattle is important, but maybe this impromptu road trip is too. A chance to clear my head, to breathe outside the suffocating walls of my Chicago office, and get in some miles with the car I love but have kept mostly in the parking garage during my four-year tenure with the firm after moving to Chicago.

The sun dips lower on the Montana horizon, and I blink, momentarily dazzled by the beauty. I notice something odd ahead. A shimmer in the air, like heat rising from hot asphalt, but more substantial and...sparkly?

My car passes through it before I can react. For a split second, the world seems to ripple around me. Static crackles through the radio, and goosebumps prickle along my arms.

"What the—" I start to say, but I stop talking when the car jerks violently. The engine sputters and dies, leaving me coasting to a stop on the shoulder of the road.

I sit there for a moment, stunned. The sudden silence is deafening after hours of road noise. I turn the key in the ignition three times. Nothing. Not even a sputter.

"Come on, Vivi." I smack the steering wheel in frustration. I pop the hood and climb out, already knowing if the car needs more than an oil change, I'm out of luck.

I shiver as the early October wind cuts through my flannel shirt as I lift the hood. Tendrils of steam rise from the engine, carrying the acrid scent of burnt rubber. I wave my hand, dispersing the vapor, but I might as well be looking at an alien artifact. Corporate law didn't prepare me for automotive emergencies. Dad made sure I could change a tire and my own oil, but I never had much interest in learning things beyond that.

I pull out my phone, ready to call for help, but the screen remains stubbornly blank. No signal. Perfect.

With a sigh, I look up and down the road. It stretches emptily in both directions with no other vehicles in sight, but wait—there, just visible in the fading light, is a sign. I squint, making out the words: "Welcome to Evershift Haven."

I glance back at my useless car, then to the sign, weighing my options. The smart thing would be to wait for another car to pass by, but how long might that take? And something about that shimmering barrier I passed through nags at me. What if no one else comes along?

Decision made, I grab my purse and jacket from the car. I make sure it's locked—more out of habit than any real concern—and start walking toward the sign. The gravel crunches beneath my feet, and a cool breeze rustles through the trees lining the road.

With some walking, I step into Evershift Haven, and my jaw drops. The town square before me is a riot of color and activity, unlike anything I've ever seen. Cobblestone streets wind between quaint buildings that look like they've stepped out of a fairy tale, complete with gingerbread trim and windows that glow with warm, inviting light.

My first thought is that I've stumbled onto a movie set. Elaborate Halloween decorations adorn every surface, from intricately carved jack-o'-lanterns grinning from windowsills to garlands of autumn leaves and twinkling lights strung between lamp posts. The air is thick with the scent of cinnamon, pumpkin spice, and something else—a hint of ozone, like the air after a thunderstorm.

"Excuse me," says a melodious voice. I turn to see a woman who resembles a tree, with hair that seems to be made from leaves. Her makeup is flawless, giving her skin an almost iridescent sheen. "You look a bit lost. Can I help you find your way?"

I blink, trying to process the elaborate costume. "I... my car broke down on the highway. Is there a mechanic in town?"

She nods. "Oh, you'll want 'Throk's Mystical Motors.' It's just down Whimsical Way, past 'The Enchanted Espresso.' You can't miss it—it's the building with the floating wrenches out front."

I nod, not quite processing her words. Floating wrenches? These people really go all out with their decorations. "Thank you, Miss...?"

"Willow," she says with a bright smile. "Willow Whisperwind. I teach yoga at Fae Fitness. You should stop by for a class while you're in town."

"Right, thanks," I say, still overwhelmed. As I start down the street she indicated, I admire the attention to detail. Every shop seems to be in on the act, with names like "The Whimsical Wardrobe" and "Beastly Bites." The signs are hand-painted works of art, swinging gently in the breeze.

People bustle past me, all in elaborate costumes. There's a man with blue skin and gills painted on his neck, carrying a trident. A group of children run by, their laughter tinkling like bells, wearing outfits that make them look like tiny woodland creatures. One even has a tail that seems to swish on its own.

I shake my head, impressed by the commitment to the illusion. It's only early October, but clearly, this town takes its Halloween celebrations seriously. The special effects must cost a fortune.

As I walk, I notice more details that add to the magical atmosphere. The streetlamps flicker to life as the sun sets, but instead of a normal glow, they emit a soft, multicolored light that dances and shifts. The effect is mesmerizing, casting ever-changing shadows that seem to move with a life of their own.

The smell of coffee draws me toward a cozy-looking café. The sign above the door reads "The Enchanted Espresso" in swirling, glowing script. Through the window, cups float through the air, gently descending to tables where patrons sit. One of the patrons appears to have rabbit ears poking out of her hair, while another has skin that sparkles like it's dusted with glitter.

I push open the door, and a little bell tinkles overhead. The interior is warm and inviting, with plush armchairs and tables that look like they're made from polished tree stumps. The wallpaper catches my eye. It seems to be shifting and changing, the patterns swirling and reforming as I watch.

"Welcome to 'The Enchanted Espresso,'" calls out a cheerful voice. I turn to see a woman behind the counter, her hair a wild mane of curls that seem to defy gravity. She's wearing a pointed hat and a dress that shimmers with constellations. "What can I brew up for you today? Our special is the Metamorphosis Mocha—guaranteed to bring out your wild side."

I approach the counter, still taking in the incredible decor. "Just a regular coffee, please. Black."

The barista—her nametag reads "Bella"—looks a bit disappointed. "Are you sure? Not even a sprinkle of our Pixie Dust sweetener?"

I shake my head. "No, thank you. Just regular coffee."

As Bella prepares my drink, I ask, "So, does the whole town get into the Halloween spirit this early?"

Bella looks at me quizzically. "Halloween? Oh, you must be new here. Evershift Haven is always like this. We're a town that celebrates magic all year round, and the town shifts with the holidays and seasons."

I nod, playing along. "Right, of course. It's very impressive."

Bella beams. "Isn't it? Oh, here's your coffee. That'll be three gold pieces."

I blink. "Gold pieces?"

She laughs. "I'm just teasing. Four dollars, please."

I hand over the money, relieved to be dealing with something normal. As I take my coffee, I notice the cup seems unusually warm, almost vibrating in my hand. The liquid inside swirls with tiny golden flecks that catch the light.

"Enjoy your stay in Evershift Haven," she says with a wink. "And don't be afraid to embrace a little magic while you're here."

I nod, still bewildered, and make my way back out onto the street. The sun has fully set now, and the town seems to have come even more alive. The twinkling lights in the trees pulse gently, almost like a heartbeat. In the distance, I hear what sounds like a clock chiming, but the melody is unlike anything I've ever heard before. It's ethereal and haunting.

As I sip my coffee—which tastes richer and more complex than any coffee I've had before—I continue my search for the mechanic. The street signs are no help. They seem to change every time I look at them. One moment I'm on "Whimsical Way," and the next, it's "Enchantment Avenue."

I pass by a storefront with a window full of books. The sign above reads "Evershift Library" in letters that appear to be formed from living vines. Through the window, I see books floating off shelves and pages turning on their own. An elderly man with long, pointed ears is gesturing animatedly to a group of children as the air around him shimmers and an image appears—a dragon, seemingly made of mist and starlight, that coils around the room.

I shake my head, impressed by the holographic technology. This town must have some serious funding to pull off effects like these.

As I turn a corner, I finally spot what must be the mechanic's shop. Wrenches float in front of the building. They spin lazily in the air, catching the light from the multicolored streetlamps. The sign reads "Throk's Mystical Motors" in letters that look like they're made of gears and pistons, constantly shifting and realigning.

I push open the door and discover the interior is a marvel of organized chaos. Tools line the walls, but they're unlike any tools I've ever seen. Some pulse with an inner light, while others hover slightly above their hooks. In one corner, a car is suspended in mid-air, surrounded by a faint blue glow.

"Be right with you," says a gravelly voice from somewhere in the back.

I wait, taking in more details. A calendar on the wall shows unfamiliar months—"Frostfall" and "Bloomrise" among them. The clock above it has thirteen hours and hands that move in what seems to be random directions.

Heavy footsteps approach from the back of the shop, and I gasp as a towering figure emerges from behind a partially disassembled hovering motorcycle. He's massive, easily seven feet tall, with broad shoulders that barely fit through the doorway. His skin is a deep forest green, covered in intricate darker green markings that swirl across his exposed arms and neck. Small tusks protrude slightly from his lower lip, and his amber eyes seem to glow in the shop's dim lighting.

I forgot how to breathe for a second. This has to be the most elaborate costume I've ever seen. The attention to detail is incredible, from the pointed ears adorned with multiple hoop piercings to the long black hair tied back in a messy bun. Even his beard looks real, neatly trimmed and peppered with what appear to be tiny braids.

He wipes his hands on a grease-stained rag as he approaches, a friendly smile revealing more of those impressive tusks. "Welcome to Mystical Motors. I'm Throk Ironheart. What can I do for you?"

His voice is deep and rumbling, with an accent I can't quite place. I swallow hard, trying to regain my composure. "Hi, I'm Suzette. My car broke down on the highway just outside of town. I was hoping you could take a look at it?"

He nods. "Of course. Where exactly did it happen?" I describe the location, and his brow gathers slightly. "Ah, near the town border. That can be tricky sometimes. The barrier doesn't always play nicely with human technology, especially if Grizelda is distracted."

I blink, unsure how to respond to that. He must be really committed to this fantasy roleplay thing.

"Let me grab my toolkit, and we'll head out there." He turns to retrieve a battered metal box from a nearby workbench. As he bends over, I admire the way his muscles ripple beneath his formfitting T-shirt. It has to be some kind of bodysuit, right? No one is actually built like that.

I wonder what he looks like underneath all that elaborate makeup and prosthetics. With his height, he could easily be a professional wrestler or athlete, but then I imagine him as a pale, skinny guy hunched over a computer, obsessively perfecting every detail of this costume for hours on end. The mental image is so at odds with the imposing figure before me that I have to stifle a giggle.

Throk turns back to me, toolkit in hand. "Something amusing?"

I shake my head quickly. "No, sorry. Just admiring your costume. It's really impressive."

He tilts his head, confusion evident in his expression. "Costume? This is just how I look."

I nod, playing along. "Right, of course. My mistake."

He leads me outside to a rugged-looking jeep parked beside the shop. The vehicle seems to hover a few inches off the ground, wheels conspicuously absent. I blink hard. The special effects in this town are starting to mess with my head.

We drive toward where I left my car as he asks questions about what happened. I describe the shimmering barrier I passed through, and the way my car suddenly died. He listens intently, occasionally nodding.

"Sounds like a classic case of magical interference," he says when we pull up behind my stranded vehicle. "The barrier between your world and ours can sometimes short out non-enchanted technology."

I laugh nervously. "Right, magical interference. Of course."

He gives me an odd look but doesn't comment. He pops the hood of my car and leans in, his massive frame dwarfing the engine compartment. I can't resist staring at his back, marveling at the seamless blend between the green "skin" and his clothing. How long must it take to apply all that makeup?

After a few minutes of tinkering, accompanied by muttered words in a language I don't recognize, he straightens up. "The good news is, I can fix it. The bad news, is I'll need to order some special parts. It'll take about a week to get everything sorted out."

My heart sinks. "A week? I have a conference in Seattle in three days."

His expression is sympathetic. "I'm sorry, but that's the fastest I can do. Mundane parts won't work with the residual magic from the barrier. We'll need to get some components from the 'Enchanted Emporium,' and Grizelda can be...particular about rush orders."

I let out a ragged breath. "This is insane. Look, I appreciate the commitment to...whatever this is, but I really need my car fixed. Isn't there a regular mechanic in the next town over?"

Throk's brow furrows, and for a moment, I swear his ears twitch. "Suzette, I'm not sure you understand. This isn't a game or a costume. Evershift Haven is a magical town, hidden from the human world. The reason your car won't start is because it's been affected by real magic."

I stare at him, waiting for the punchline. When it doesn't come, I laugh nervously. "Okay, you got me. This is all very impressive, but I need to get to Seattle, so if you could just point me toward a real mechanic—"

He scowls. "I assure you, this is a real magical problem. The barrier between our worlds—"

I hold up a hand, cutting him off. "Look, I get it. It's fine for the tourists, but I just need my car fixed. Can we drop the act and talk about this seriously?"

His shoulders slump slightly, and he lets out a heavy sigh. The tusks protruding from his lower lip catch the fading light as he speaks. "I understand this is difficult to accept, but I promise you, I'm being entirely serious."

I cross my arms, frustration mounting. "Seriously? You expect me to believe this town is actually magical? That you're really some kind of...orc mechanic?"

He nods. "That's exactly what I'm telling you."

I pinch the bridge of my nose, trying to stave off the headache I feel building. "Okay, fine. Let's say, for argument's sake, this is all real. How long will it actually take to fix my car?"

Throk's expression softens slightly. "As I said before, it'll take about a week to get the necessary parts and perform the repairs. I'm truly sorry, but there's no faster way to do it properly."

I glance at my watch, then back at my stranded car. The reality of my situation starts to sink in. "A week? But my conference... What am I supposed to do for a whole week?"

Throk scratches his beard thoughtfully, the small braids woven into it swaying lightly. "There's a lovely bed and breakfast in town. 'The Moonlit Inn.' The owners, Etienne and Crystal, are wonderful hosts. They could set you up with a room while we work on your car."

I let out a long breath. A week in this bizarre town? With all these people in elaborate costumes, pretending to be magical creatures? It sounds like a nightmare, but what choice do I have?

"Fine," I say with resignation. "I guess I don't have much choice. Can you please give me a ride back to town?"

Throk nods, flashing a small mile. "Of course. I'll drop you off at the inn myself."

After getting my bag, which is mostly work wear, we climb back into his strange, wheel-less jeep, and I marvel at the dedication these people have to their charade. The vehicle hums to life without a key, and we begin to glide smoothly back toward town.

The trip is mostly silent, with Throk occasionally pointing out landmarks. "That's the Whispering Woods," he says, gesturing to a dense forest, where the trees seem to sway despite the lack of wind. "And over there is Luminous Lagoon. It's beautiful at night when the water glows."

I nod politely, still convinced this is all an elaborate show for tourists. When we enter the town proper, the lights seem even more vibrant than before. The streets are busy with people in fantastical costumes, going about their evening as if it's perfectly normal to have wings or horns or blue skin.

We pull up in front of a Victorian-style mansion, its windows glowing with warm, inviting light. The sign out front reads "Moonlit Inn" in elegant, swirling script that shimmers and changes color as I watch.

He helps me with my bag, carrying it effortlessly up the steps to the inn's front door. We approach, and the door swings open on its own, revealing a tall, impossibly handsome man with pale skin and slicked-back black hair.

"Ah, Throk. What a pleasant surprise," says the man, his voice smooth and cultured with a faint hint of perhaps a French accent. He sees me, and a charming smile spreads across his face. "And who might this lovely guest be?"

Throk introduces us. "Etienne, this is Suzette. She ran into some car trouble at the town border. Suzette, this is Etienne St. John, one of the owners of 'Moonlit Inn.'"

Etienne bows slightly, his movements graceful and fluid. "A pleasure to meet you, Suzette. Welcome to our humble establishment. I do hope you'll find your stay with us enchanting."

I force a smile, trying to match his politeness despite my increasing irritation with this whole situation. "Thank you. I might be staying for about a week while my car gets fixed."

Etienne's eyebrows rise slightly. "A week? How delightful. We so rarely get to truly know our guests. Crystal will be thrilled."

As if on cue, a willowy woman with long auburn hair and violet eyes appears beside Etienne. Her skin seems to glow with an inner light, and she moves with the same otherworldly grace as her partner. "Did I hear we have a new guest?" she asks, her voice musical and light.

Etienne nods. "Indeed, my dear. This is Suzette. She'll be staying with us for a week while Throk works his magic on her vehicle."

Crystal beams. "Oh, how wonderful. We'll make sure you have a magical stay, Suzette."

I smile weakly, wondering what I've gotten myself into. "Thank you. That's very kind."

Throk sets down my bag in the entryway. "I should be getting back to the shop. Suzette, I'll keep you updated on the progress with your car. Don't hesitate to stop by if you need anything."

I nod, suddenly reluctant to see him go. Despite the ridiculousness of his costume and claims of magic, Throk has been the most normal part of this entire experience so far. As he turns to leave, I say, "Throk? Thanks for your help."

He gives me a warm smile. "My pleasure. Enjoy your stay in Evershift Haven. Who knows? You might discover some magic of your own."

With that, he's gone, leaving me alone with the impossibly perfect innkeepers. Etienne picks up my bag with ease, while Crystal links her arm through mine.

"Come, dear," she says, leading me toward the stairs. "Let's get you settled in. I have a feeling you're going to love room Thirteen. It has the most marvelous view of the Celestial Clock Tower."

Crystal chatters away while we climb, pointing out various features of the inn. "The paintings? Oh, they're all originals. Some of them are quite mischievous, always switching places when no one's looking, and that suit of armor? It likes to go for walks at night, but don't worry, it's quite friendly."

I nod along, marveling at the level of detail in their act. The wallpaper seems to shift and change when we pass, flowers blooming and vines curling in our wake. The carpet beneath our feet is impossibly plush, and I swear it's adjusting to cradle each step perfectly.

We reach the third floor, and she leads me down a hallway lined with doors of various shapes and sizes. Some are tall and narrow while others are short and wide. One appears to be made entirely of shimmering water, while another looks like it's crafted from living vines constantly growing and then pruning itself.

"Here we are," she says, stopping in front of a perfectly ordinary-looking door with the number "13" in gleaming gold. "Your home away from home."

She pushes open the door, and I step inside, my jaw dropping despite myself. The room is far larger than it should be given the size of the building. A massive four-poster bed dominates one wall, draped in shimmering fabrics that changes color as I watch. The far wall is entirely glass, offering a breathtaking view of the town and, true to Crystal's word, an ornate clock tower that gleams in the moonlight.

"The wardrobe is over there." Crystal gestures to an imposing piece of furniture that looks like it stepped out of a fairy tale. "The bathroom has all the usual amenities, plus a few magical extras. Oh, and the desk will provide any writing materials or books you might want—just ask it nicely."

I turn to her, overwhelmed. "This is incredible."

She waves a hand dismissively. "Thank you. You're our guest, and we want you to be comfortable."

"I'm sure I will be." I wonder how much this is going to put on my credit card, and that reminds me to make sure I give them my personal, not business, card when I register. I can't expect the firm to foot the bill for my impromptu layover due to Vivi's faulty wiring, or whatever is wrong it the car.

"You must be tired after your long day. Why don't you get some rest? Food is served whenever you're hungry. The dining room has a way of knowing."

With that cryptic statement, she glides out of the room, leaving me alone in this impossible space. I sit heavily on the edge of the bed, my mind spinning. The mattress seems to mold perfectly to my body, offering just the right amount of support.

I shake my head, trying to clear it. This is all so elaborate and convincing, but it can't be real. Magic isn't real. There has to be a rational explanation for all of this.

I ponder this, glancing at the clock tower visible through the window. The hands are moving in ways that defy logic, spinning backward and forward before sometimes stopping altogether, and yet, somehow, I know exactly what time it is.

I flop back on the bed, staring up at the canopy. How am I going to survive a week in this madhouse? Candi is the gamer in our family, and the one into LARPing and conventions. I'm more mundane.

As my eyelids close, weariness finally catching up with me, I wonder what if there's more to Evershift Haven than meets the eye? What if, against all logic and reason, magic really is real? With these unsettling thoughts swirling in my mind, I slip into a deep, dreamless sleep.

Chapter 2

I OPEN MY EYES TO AN unfamiliar ceiling, momentarily disoriented. The events of yesterday flood back—my car breaking down, the strange town of Evershift Haven, and the even stranger inhabitants.

Sitting up, I reach for my phone on the nightstand. The screen shows no service, which is odd considering I had a signal yesterday. I try connecting to the inn's Wi-Fi, but it refuses to work. With a sigh, I get out of bed and dress quickly in yesterday's clothes, making a mental note to find a place to buy some essentials later.

My bag is filled with a pair of pajamas I was too tired to put on last night and business attire that I don't want to wear all week. I'm wearing one of my only two casual outfits, and the other is in a plastic bag in my trunk, since I wore it yesterday and had planned to get laundry service at the hotel I never reached last night.

I head downstairs, hoping to find a landline to make calls. The lobby is empty, save for a sleek black cat lounging on the front desk. Its yellow eyes track my movements as I approach.

"Good morning," I say, feeling slightly foolish for addressing a cat. "I don't suppose you know where I can find a phone?"

The cat yawns, revealing sharp teeth, then hops off the desk. It pads over to an ornate side table, where an old-fashioned rotary phone sits. The cat looks at me expectantly.

"Right. Thanks," I mutter, picking up the receiver. To my surprise, there's a dial tone. I punch in Candice's number from memory, praying she'll pick up.

After several rings, my sister's cheerful voice comes through. "Hello?"

"Candice, it's me," I say, glad to hear a familiar voice.

"Suz? Where are you calling from? The number didn't show up on my caller ID."

I laugh nervously. "You wouldn't believe me if I told you. My car broke down in this weird little town called Evershift Haven. I'm stuck here for a week while they order parts."

"Oh, no. Are you okay? Do you need me to come get you?"

"No, no, I'm fine. Just confused. This place is really strange, Candi. Everyone's acting like they're magical creatures or something. I think it might be some kind of tourist trap, but it's intense."

There's a pause on the other end of the line. "Evershift Haven, you said?"

"Yeah, have you heard of it?"

Another pause. "No, and an Internet search turns up no results, but it sounds interesting. Are you sure you're okay there?"

I glance around the empty lobby, seeing the cat, who's still watching me intently. "I think so. The people seem nice enough, just eccentric. I'll be careful, I promise."

"Okay, keep me updated, and, Suz? Try to have some fun, okay? You work too hard."

I roll my eyes but can't help smiling. "I'll try. Love you, sis."

"Love you too. Be safe."

As I hang up, the cat has moved closer, its tail swishing back and forth. "I don't suppose you know Erik Thompson's direct line at Hartwell, Pierce, and Associates?" I ask with a hint of silliness.

To my shock, the cat meows and bats at the phone with its paw. The rotary dial spins on its own, clicking into place for each number. When it stops, I hesitantly pick up the receiver again.

A gruff voice answers. "Erik Thompson."

I swallow hard, trying to process what just happened with the phone. "Er, hi, Erik. It's Suzette Winters."

"Winters? Aren't you supposed to be at the conference in Seattle?" His tone is already accusatory, and I feel my shoulders tense.

"That's why I'm calling. My car broke down on the way there. I'm stuck in a small town for repairs. I won't be able to make it."

There's a heavy sigh on the other end. "Winters, this conference was crucial. The networking alone could have brought in several new high-profile clients."

I bite my tongue, resisting the urge to point out I'm not the only lawyer at the firm capable of networking. "I understand, Erik. I'm sorry for the inconvenience. I'll make it up to the firm when I return."

"See that you do, and I expect you to work remotely while you're stranded in...where did you say you were?"

"Evershift Haven," I say, my jaw clenching. Speaking to the senior partner always reminds me how much I hate my job.

There's a pause. "Never heard of it. Regardless, I want daily progress reports on the Henderson case. No excuses."

"Of course," I say, my free hand curling into a fist as I resist the urge to ask about the Henderson case. I've never heard of it, so it's probably been assigned to one of his hundred underlings, and he has no idea who I actually am. "Is there anything else?"

"Just get back here as soon as possible. We can't afford to have our associates gallivanting around small towns when there's work to be done."

The line goes dead before I can respond. I slam down the receiver, annoyance boiling over. "Insufferable, micromanaging..." I mutter a string of colorful expletives under my breath.

The cat meows sympathetically, rubbing against my leg. I reach down to scratch behind its ears. "Thanks for the help with the phone," I say. "Though I'm not sure how you did that."

"Whiskers is an empath," says Etienne from behind me. "He's also quite talented with numbers."

I blink, trying to formulate a response that doesn't make me sound crazy...or imply my host is. "Right. Of course. Whiskers the...phone-dialing, empathic cat."

Etienne smiles, revealing perfectly white teeth that seem just a bit too sharp. "I hope your calls went well? You seemed distressed at the end there."

"Just work stuff. Nothing I can't handle."

"Ah, the trials of the mortal workforce," says Etienne with a knowing nod. "Perhaps a bit of breakfast would help? There's a lovely spread in the dining room."

My stomach growls at the mention of food, reminding me I haven't eaten since yesterday afternoon. "That sounds great, actually. Thank you."

Etienne gestures for me to follow him, and I do, with Whiskers trotting along beside us. The dining room is a grand space with high ceilings and large windows overlooking a lush garden. A long table set with an array of dishes instantly makes my mouth water.

Crystal appears from a side door, carrying a steaming pot of what smells like the most delicious coffee I've ever encountered. "Good morning, Suzette. I hope you slept well?"

"I did, thank you." I take a seat at the table. "This all looks amazing."

She beams at me as she pours coffee into a delicate china cup. "I'm so glad. Please, help yourself to anything you'd like. We have traditional fare as well as some local specialties."

I eye the spread before me. Alongside familiar items like scrambled eggs and toast, there are dishes I don't recognize. A bowl of what looks like oatmeal shimmers with an iridescent sheen. Another plate holds what appear to be perfectly normal bacon strips, but they're slowly changing color as I watch.

Deciding to play it safe, I reach for the eggs and toast. As I eat, Etienne and Crystal move about the room, seeming to float rather than walk. Whiskers hops up onto the chair next to me, watching me with those unnerving yellow eyes.

"So, Suzette," says Crystal, refilling my coffee cup without me asking, "What are your plans for the day? Evershift Haven has so much to offer."

I swallow a bite of toast. "I should probably check in with Throk about my car, and I need to pick up some clothes and toiletries since I didn't pack for an extended stay."

Etienne nods approvingly. "Excellent choices. Might I suggest the 'Whimsical Wardrobe' for your clothing needs? Madam Karvin has an uncanny ability to stock exactly what her customers require."

"And don't forget to stop by the 'Enchanted Emporium' for any other necessities," says his wife. "Grizelda keeps a wonderfully eclectic inventory."

I nod, making mental notes. Despite the strangeness of it all, I'm looking forward to exploring the town. Maybe Candice was right—I could use a little fun, even if it's in this bizarre place.

As I finish my breakfast, a thought occurs to me. "Is there somewhere in town I could set up to do some work? I need to review some case files."

Etienne and Crystal exchange a glance. "The Evershift Library might suit your needs," he says. "It's a quiet establishment, perfect for concentration, but human Internet can be spotty here. Too much—"

"Let me guess...magical interference?" I say with a smile, recalling Throk's words yesterday.

"Precisely."

"That might be why my phone isn't working today." Either that, or I'm in rural Montana, which probably has spotty cell service, but where's the fun in the town saying that when they're working so hard to create this illusion? I stand up. "I guess I'll head out then. Thank you both for breakfast. It was delicious."

Moments later, I step out of the "Moonlit Inn" and into the strange world of Evershift Haven. The air is crisp and clean, carrying the scent of flowers and something else I can't quite place—a hint of spice or maybe ozone. It's unlike anything I've smelled before.

As I adjust the strap of my purse, movement catches my eye. Through the inn's front window, I spot a figure gliding across the lobby. It's a woman in an old-fashioned maid's uniform, her form slightly translucent. I gasp as she approaches the solid wall—and passes right through it.

I blink hard. When I look again, she's gone.

"It's just special effects," I mutter to myself, shaking my head. "Some kind of hologram or projection. There's got to be a logical explanation."

Despite my attempts at rationalization, I'm not entirely convinced as I turn away from the inn, determined to focus on my errands for the day.

I spot a sign for the "Whimsical Wardrobe" and head in that direction. As I walk, I notice more oddities. A man reading a newspaper on a bench has horns sprouting from his forehead. A woman watering flowers outside her shop has skin that shimmers with an iridescent green hue.

"It's all makeup and prosthetics," I tell myself firmly. "Probably some kind of festival or tourist attraction."

The bell above the "Whimsical Wardrobe's" door chimes as I enter. The shop is larger inside than it appeared from the street, filled with racks of clothing in every color imaginable. Some of the fabrics seem to shift and change as I look at them.

"Welcome, dear." I turn to see a tall, elegantly dressed woman approaching. Her hair is a vibrant purple, styled in an elaborate updo that defies gravity. "I'm Madam Karvin. How may I assist you today?"

"I, uh, need some clothes," I say, feeling a bit overwhelmed. "I'm stuck in town for a week and didn't pack enough."

Madam Karvin smiles. "Marvelous. I have just the thing. Or rather, I will have just the thing." She snaps her fingers, and several hangers float off the racks, drifting toward us.

I take an involuntary step back. "How are you doing that?"

She winks at me. "Magic, of course. Let's see what we have here."

The floating clothes arrange themselves in front of me. There's a practical yet stylish pantsuit, several blouses, a pair of jeans, and a couple of dresses. All in my size, and all in colors I would typically choose for myself.

"These are perfect," I say, reaching out to touch a silky blouse. "But how did you—"

"The 'Wardrobe' knows what you need," says Madam Karvin enigmatically. "Why don't you try them on? The fitting room is right over there."

I gather the clothes and head to the fitting room she indicated. As I change, I'm impressed at how well everything fits. It's as if they were tailored specifically for me.

When I emerge, Madam Karvin is waiting with a pair of comfortable yet stylish flats and a small selection of accessories. "To complete the look," she says with a flourish.

I check the price tags, bracing myself for the cost of such personalized service. To my surprise, the prices are quite reasonable. "I'll take it all."

As Madam Karvin rings up my purchase, I glance around the shop again. A mannequin in the corner catches my attention. It seems to be moving slightly, adjusting its pose. "Did that mannequin just move?" I ask, unable to keep the disbelief out of my voice.

Madam Karvin looks over her shoulder. "Oh, that's just Stitch. He likes to keep things interesting. Stitch, darling, say hello to our guest."

The mannequin turns its head toward me and waves.

I wave back automatically, then shake my head. "I'm sorry, but how is this possible? Is it animatronics?"

Madam Karvin laughs, a tinkling sound like wind chimes. "Oh, my dear. You're new to Evershift Haven, aren't you? There's no need for animatronics when you have magic."

I open my mouth to argue, to insist magic isn't real, but the words die on my tongue. How else can I explain everything I've seen since arriving in this town? "Right," I say weakly. "Magic. Of course."

Madam Karvin hands me my bags with a sympathetic smile. "It can be a lot to take in at first, but you'll get used to it. Evershift Haven has a way of opening one's mind to new possibilities."

I thank her and leave the shop, my head spinning. The street outside seems even more fantastical now. A group of what appear to be fairies flits past, their wings catching the sunlight. A large, furry creature that could be a yeti is carefully arranging produce at a market stall.

I draw in a deep breath, trying to center myself. "Okay, Suzette. You're a rational person. There has to be a logical explanation for all of this."

Continuing my walk, I soon spot a shop with a sign that seems to be morphing before my eyes. One moment, it reads "Enchanted Emporium" in flowing script, and the next, it's "Magical Miscellany" in bold block letters.

The shop's interior is a riot of color and strange smells. Shelves stretch up to the ceiling, crammed with an assortment of items I can't even begin to identify. Bottles of liquids in every hue imaginable line one wall, while another displays an array of crystals and gemstones.

"Hello, there," says a cheerful voice. A woman with pale green skin emerges from behind a towering stack of books. Her wild mane of silver-streaked purple hair seems to move on its own, and her eyes sparkle with an otherworldly purple light. "Welcome to the 'Enchanted Emporium.' I'm Grizelda. What can I help you find today?"

"Just some basic toiletries," I say, trying not to stare at her hair. "Toothbrush, toothpaste, and that sort of thing."

"Of course. Let's see what we have." She begins to rummage through drawers and cabinets, pulling out items and muttering to herself. I catch phrases like "No, no, too strong for a beginner" and "Ooh, this might be fun."

Finally, she presents me with a small basket. "Here we are. A basic toiletry kit for the discerning visitor to Evershift Haven."

I peer into the basket. There's a toothbrush that seems to be made of some kind of iridescent material, a tube of toothpaste labeled "Minty Fresh Breath (Now With Fifty Percent Less Chance of Temporary Invisibility)," a bar of soap that's gently pulsing with a soft blue light, and a bottle of shampoo that claims to "Bring Out Your Inner Glow (Literal Glowing May Occur)."

"Um," I say, not quite sure how to respond. "Do you have anything a bit more normal?"

She looks puzzled. "Normal? Oh, you mean mundane. I'm sorry, dear, but we don't get much call for that sort of thing here in Evershift Haven. These are all perfectly safe for human use. Err, mostly safe. Just don't use the toothpaste more than twice a day, and you should be fine."

I nod along, as if what she's saying makes perfect sense. "Right. Of course. How much do I owe you?"

As she rings up my purchase, I notice a plant on the counter. Its leaves are a deep purple, and it seems to be humming? One of the leaves reaches out and gently strokes her arm.

"Oh, stop that, you flirt," she says to the plant, patting its leaves affectionately. She turns back to me with a smile. "Sorry about that. Violet here gets a bit overly friendly sometimes."

I hand over my credit card, half-expecting it not to work in this strange place despite working in the clothing store. Thankfully, the transaction goes through without a hitch.

"Is there anything else you need?" she asks as she hands me my receipt. "Love potion? Lucky charm? We're having a sale on crystal balls—great for beginners."

"No, thank you," I say quickly. "This is plenty for now."

As I turn to leave, she calls out, "Oh, and dear? A word of advice—try to keep an open mind. Evershift Haven has a way of surprising people, especially those who think they've got it all figured out."

I nod, not trusting myself to speak, and hurry out of the shop. The street outside feels almost normal in comparison to the chaos of the Emporium.

I check my watch, realizing it's already past noon. My stomach growls, reminding me I haven't eaten since breakfast. I spot a cozy-looking café across the street and decide to grab a quick lunch before heading to the library to get some work done.

As I cross the street, a gust of wind blows through the square. To my amazement, the leaves swirling in the breeze seem to form patterns—for a moment, I swear I see them spell out "Welcome to Evershift Haven" before dispersing.

I shake my head, wondering if I'm starting to hallucinate from stress. "Get it together, Suzette," I mutter to myself. "You're a rational, level-headed lawyer. There has to be a logical explanation for all of this."

As I reach for the café door, I wonder if maybe I need to start expanding my definition of what's possible.

Chapter 3

AFTER LUNCH, I STROLL through Evershift Haven's town square. The quaint cobblestone streets and Tudor-style buildings seem plucked from a storybook, yet there's an undeniable vibrancy that pulses through the air. Shopkeepers bustle about, preparing their storefronts for what appears to be an upcoming festival.

I notice a familiar figure standing in the center of the square. Grizelda, the eccentric proprietor of the "Enchanted Emporium," waves her arms in sweeping gestures. I blink, certain I'm imagining things. Colorful banners and strings of twinkling lights float in mid-air, positioning themselves along storefronts and across the square.

"No," I whisper, shaking my head. "This isn't possible." I squeeze my eyelids shut, count to ten, and open them again. The decorations continue their aerial dance, guided by Grizelda's movements.

"Okay, Suzette," I whisper to myself. "You're hallucinating. Maybe that coffee was laced with something. Or you hit your head when the car broke down. There's a logical explanation for all of this."

A group of children runs past, laughing and pointing at the flying decorations. One small boy with pointed ears—clearly part of an elaborate costume—claps his hands in delight as a banner swoops low over his head.

"Ms. Greenwarth," he calls out. "Can you make the lights spell my name?"

Grizelda turns. "Of course, little Pip. Watch this."

With a flick of her wrist, a strand of lights detaches itself from the main group. It twists and turns in the air, forming letters: P-I-P.

The boy—Pip—squeals with joy, jumping up and down. His friends crowd around him, begging Grizelda to spell their names too.

I back away. This is too much. Too real. The special effects, if that's what they are, are far beyond anything I've ever seen, and everyone's acting as if it's completely normal. "I need to get out of here," I say, turning to leave the square as I collide with a solid wall of muscle, stumbling backward. Strong hands catch me before I fall.

"Whoa there, Suzette. You okay?"

I look up into Throk's eyes, noting his tusks protrude slightly when he frowns. Even in my panicked state, I notice how the sunlight catches the intricate darker green markings on his forest-green skin. "I... I..." I stammer, unable to form a coherent thought.

His frown deepens. He glances over my shoulder, then back at me. "Ah," he says softly. "First time accepting you're seeing real magic, huh?"

I laugh, a high-pitched, slightly hysterical sound. "Magic? There's no such thing as magic. This is...some kind of elaborate hoax. Or I'm going insane. Yes, that must be it. I've finally cracked under the pressure of work and—"

"Suzette," he interrupts gently. "Inhale and exhale."

Despite myself, I comply. The autumn air fills my lungs, carrying the scent of apples and cinnamon.

"Good." He nods. "I know this is a lot to take in, but I promise you're not going crazy. Everything you're seeing is real."

I shake my head vehemently. "That's impossible. Magic isn't real. People can't just float things in the air."

He chuckles, and it's a warm, rich sound that seems to vibrate through me. "In the human world, sure, but Evershift Haven isn't part of the human world. It exists in a space between realities, where magic is as natural as breathing."

I open my mouth to argue, but no words come out. How can I argue with what I'm seeing? With what everyone around me seems to accept as normal?

"Come on," he says, gently guiding me toward a nearby bench. "Let's sit down for a minute. I'll try to explain."

We settle onto the bench, and I notice absently that it's unusually comfortable for a park bench. Almost as if it's conforming to my body. "Okay," I say, taking another deep breath. "Explain."

He settles onto the bench beside me, his massive frame dwarfing mine. He takes a deep breath and stares at me. "Evershift Haven exists in a pocket dimension. It's a refuge for magical creatures and humans who've discovered their own latent magical abilities. The town's protected by a powerful enchantment that keeps it hidden from the outside world—unless Grizelda, our town witch, is distracted. Then the barrier sometimes falters for a few seconds—which is how you slipped through."

I shake my head, struggling to process his words. "Impossible. Magic isn't real."

One side of his mouth curls upward in amusement. "I understand your skepticism. It's a lot to take in, but I can prove it to you." He leans closer, and I fight the urge to sway toward him. "Watch this," he says.

To my astonishment, Throk's small tusks begin to retract into his mouth. Within seconds, they've disappeared completely, leaving him with a perfectly normal—if unusually handsome—human smile. His skin becomes bronzed brown instead of green, and he looks like a huge wrestler or athlete, reminding me of my first impression of him.

My jaw drops. "How did you do that?"

Throk grins, his tusks slowly re-emerging as his skin returns to its former green shade. "Magic. It's a glamour spell most of us learn to help blend in if we need to venture into the human world, but here in Evershift, we can be our true selves."

I reach out hesitantly, my fingers hovering near his face. "May I?"

He nods, and I gently touch the smooth green skin of his cheek, tracing the path to where his tusk emerges. It's solid, warm, and undeniably real.

"This is incredible, but why hide a whole town?"

He becomes serious. "For protection. Throughout history, magical beings have been persecuted by humans who didn't understand us. Evershift Haven was created as a safe place where we could live freely, without fear."

I think about the witch trials, the folklore of monsters and demons. Had there been truth to those stories all along? All of them usually had unpleasant endings for the so-called monsters. "Everyone here is magical?"

Throk nods. "In one way or another. Some, like me, are magical creatures. Others are humans, who've discovered their own innate magical abilities."

My mind races with questions. "And the town itself? The decorations that were floating earlier?"

"Grizelda. She's one of our most powerful witches. She helps maintain the town's magical barriers and often lends a hand with festival preparations."

I glance around the square, seeing it with a new perspective. The vibrant colors, the impossible architecture, and the subtle shimmer in the air all suddenly make sense.

"What about my car?" I ask. "You said magical interference caused it to break down?"

Throk nods. "The barrier around Evershift can sometimes disrupt technology. It's a side effect of the protection spell. I'll be able to fix it, but it'll take some specialized parts."

I slouch back on the bench, overwhelmed. "This is a lot to process."

He places a warm hand on my shoulder. "I know. Take your time. You're safe here. No one will harm you."

His touch is reassuring. Despite the fantastical nature of everything he's told me, I believe him. "So, what happens now?" I ask.

"That's up to you. You're welcome to stay in Evershift while I repair your car. Explore the town and meet the residents. Or if you prefer, we can arrange for you to leave immediately but with a dead car that will never function again in your world, since it requires magical parts. We have ways of ensuring you won't remember what you've seen here."

The thought of forgetting all this—the magic, the wonder, and the gentle orc sitting beside me—constricts my chest. "No," I say firmly. "I want to remember. I want to learn more."

His face lights up with a brilliant smile. "I was hoping you'd say that. There's so much to show you." He stands, offering me his hand. "Would you like a proper tour of Evershift Haven?"

I take his hand, gaping at how small mine looks engulfed in his green palm. "I'd love that."

We walk through the square, with me noticing details I'd missed before. A group of what I now realize are fairies flit between flower baskets, their wings shimmering in the sunlight. A stately woman with pointed ears—an elf?—nods graciously when we pass. "This is incredible. How have I never heard about any of this before?"

Throk chuckles. "The human world is very good at explaining away things it doesn't understand, and we work hard to keep our existence a secret."

We approach "The Enchanted Espresso." "Want to stop for a coffee?" he asks. "Bella's Metamorphosis Mocha is famous throughout the magical realm."

I hesitate, remembering my earlier skepticism. "Is it safe?"

He grins. "Perfectly. Though I should warn you, it might give you rabbit ears for an hour or two."

I arch a brow. "You're joking?"

"Only one way to find out." He grins, holding open the door for me.

Bella beams at us from behind the counter when we enter. "Throk. And Suzette, right? Back for another try?"

I nod, still a bit overwhelmed. "I think I'm ready for that Metamorphosis Mocha now."

Bella claps her hands gleefully. "Excellent. One Metamorphosis Mocha coming right up, and for you, Throk? The usual?"

"Please."

I watch in fascination as Bella works. She hums a melody under her breath, and the coffee beans grind themselves. Milk pours from the steamer without anyone touching it, and when she waves her hand over the finished drinks, they glow briefly before settling into swirling, iridescent patterns.

"Here you are," she says, sliding the mugs across the counter. "Enjoy."

I take a cautious sip of my mocha. The flavor explodes on my tongue—rich chocolate, hints of cinnamon and nutmeg, and something I can't quite identify. A warm tingle spreads through my body. "Oh, wow. This is amazing."

Throk grins, sipping his own drink—a deep forest green concoction that smells faintly of pine. "Just wait. The real fun's about to start."

As if on cue, there's a strange sensation on top of my head. I reach up, gasping when I feel two soft, velvety ears sprouting from my scalp and rush to the mirror hanging on the café wall. Sure enough, two adorable white rabbit ears now poke up through my hair.

Bella laughs. "They suit you. They'll fade in an hour or two unless you want to keep them longer? I can always adjust the spell."

I shake my head, watching in fascination as the ears twitch and move. "This is... I don't even know what to say."

Throk steps up behind me, his reflection grinning in the mirror. "Welcome to Evershift Haven, where magic is real, and anything is possible."

As I stare at our reflections—me with my new rabbit ears, and Throk with his green skin and tusks—I realize my life will never be the same again, and surprisingly, I'm okay with that. "So," I say, turning to face him. "What other wonders does this town have to show me?"

He looks excited. "Oh, you haven't seen anything yet. Come on. I'll show you the Whispering Woods. The trees there love to gossip about newcomers."

My new ears twitch with each sound, and I feel a sense of adventure I haven't experienced since childhood. Evershift Haven started as an accidental detour, but now I can't wait to see where this magical journey will lead.

Chapter 4

I STEP OUT OF "THE Enchanted Espresso," and Throk's massive green hand gently guides me onto the cobblestone street, his touch sending a flutter through my stomach.

"Ready for the grand tour?" He grins, his tusks glinting in the sunlight.

"As I'll ever be. Where to first?"

He points down the street. "Let's start with 'Frost's Festive Finds.' It's always an experience, no matter the season."

We make our way down the winding street, passing storefronts that seem to defy logic. One moment, we're walking past a shop with windows full of dancing cupcakes, and the next, we're peering into an apothecary, where bottles float and rearrange themselves.

"Frost's Festive Finds" appears suddenly, as if materializing out of thin air. The storefront is a riot of color and movement, with displays that shift and change every few seconds.

A tall, willowy figure with pointed ears and skin that shimmers like fresh snow greets us at the door. "Welcome to 'Frost's.' I'm Esme Greenfire. What holiday can I help you celebrate today?"

I blink in confusion. "But it's not-—"

Throk cuts me off with a gentle squeeze of my hand. "Why don't you show us what you've got for midsummer?"

The clerk claps her hands together, and suddenly, the entire store transforms. Lush greenery sprouts from every surface, fireflies dance through the air, and the scent of blooming flowers fills my nostrils.

"Oh, my." I spin in a slow circle to take it all in.

Throk chuckles, his deep voice making me tremble inside. "Pretty impressive, right?"

I nod, words failing me as I watch a miniature sun rise and set in fast motion above a display of picnic baskets.

"Care to try our midsummer mead?" Esme offers, producing two glasses filled with a golden liquid that seems to glow from within.

Throk and I accept the glasses, our fingers brushing as we reach for them. I take a sip and immediately feel warmth spreading through my body, as if I've just stepped into a sunbeam. "This is delicious," I say, licking my lips. Throk's gaze follows the movement, and a blush creeps up my cheeks.

We spend a few more minutes exploring the ever-changing displays before bidding Esme goodbye. We step back onto the street, and I realize my rabbit ears have disappeared.

"Looks like the magic's wearing off," he says, reaching out to tuck a strand of my now-normal hair behind my ear. The gentle touch sends a spark through me.

"Where to next?" I ask, my voice a little breathless.

Throk grins mischievously. "How about we check out 'Fae Fitness?' They've got some pretty unique workout equipment."

I raise an eyebrow. "Are you saying I need to exercise?"

He laughs, holding up his hands in mock surrender. "Not at all. Just thought you might enjoy seeing trolls and dryads on treadmills."

I laugh at the mental image. "Lead the way."

While strolling, I gravitate closer to Throk, drawn to his warmth and the sense of safety he provides in this strange new world. Our hands brush again, and this time, neither of us pulls away.

"Fae Fitness" looms before us in a building that seems to be made of living trees and shimmering crystal. Through the windows, I see beings of all shapes and sizes engaged in various forms of exercise.

A massive figure emerges from the front door, ducking to avoid hitting his head on the frame. His skin is gray and craggy, like living stone, with a bald head, and he has a friendly grin that seems at odds with his intimidating size. "Throk. Good to see you, buddy," booms the giant, clapping Throk on the back with enough force to stagger a normal man. Throk barely moves. "Who's your friend?"

"Atlas, this is Suzette." Throk introduces us. "Suzette, meet Atlas Mountainheart, owner of 'Fae Fitness' and married to Grizelda."

I extend my hand, which is promptly engulfed by Atlas's massive palm. "Nice to meet you," I say, trying not to wince at his enthusiastic handshake.

"Care for a tour?" Atlas offers, gesturing toward the gym.

We follow him inside, where I'm immediately struck by the bizarre sight of magical creatures working out. A group of pixies flutter around a miniature obstacle course, while a minotaur bench-presses what looks like a small boulder.

"And here's our pride and joy," he says, leading us to a row of treadmills. "Watch this."

He steps onto one and presses a button. Suddenly, the area around the treadmill shimmers and transforms. Atlas is now running through a lush jungle, complete with chattering monkeys and colorful birds flying overhead.

"That's incredible," I say as he navigates around a fallen log that isn't really there.

"Want to try?" asks Throk.

I narrow my pupils at him. "You're on."

We each claim a treadmill, and I select a beach scene from the options. As I start to jog, I'm amazed by how real it all feels—the sand beneath my feet, the salty breeze on my face, and even the sound of waves crashing nearby.

I glance over at Throk, who's running through what appears to be a volcanic landscape, leaping over lava flows and dodging falling rocks. His muscles ripple with each movement, and I stare longer than is strictly necessary.

When he catches me looking, he flashes a grin that makes my heart skip a beat. "Enjoying the view?"

I blush furiously but manage to say, "Just making sure you don't trip and fall into a volcano."

We continue our workouts, playfully teasing each other as we go. By the time we step off the treadmills, we're both breathless and laughing.

"That was actually really fun," I say when we part from Atlas and head outside.

Throk nods, wiping sweat from his brow. "Glad you enjoyed it. How about we cool off with some ice cream?"

My ears perk up at the suggestion. "Ice cream sounds perfect. Lead the way."

As we walk toward our next destination, I'm surprised by how quickly I've adapted to this magical world. Just yesterday, I was a skeptical lawyer focused solely on my career. Now, I'm strolling down a street filled with impossible things, my hand occasionally brushing against that of a handsome orc mechanic.

"The Sorcerer's Scoop" comes into view, a whimsical building that looks like it's made entirely of waffle cone. Multicolored smoke puffs from a chimney shaped like an ice cream swirl, and the air around us suddenly smells of sugar and vanilla.

A jovial voice booms from inside when we approach. "Welcome. Come in and cool your heels."

We enter to find a massive figure behind the counter, easily seven feet tall with pale blue skin and a beard that sparkles like fresh snow. Despite his intimidating size, his eyes twinkle with warmth and mischief.

He introduces himself with a flourish. "Galileo Coldborn, at your service. What can I get for you lovebirds today?"

I start to protest that we're not a couple, but Throk speaks first. "What do you recommend, Galileo?"

The frost giant grins, revealing teeth that look suspiciously like icicles. "Why, the Chameleon Crunch, of course. It's our specialty."

Before I can ask what makes it special, Galileo scoops out two generous portions of what looks like ordinary vanilla ice cream. He hands us each a cone, and I take a tentative lick. Immediately, my tongue tingles, and I watch in amazement as my hair begins to change color, shifting through the rainbow like a kaleidoscope.

Throk laughs, his own hair now a vibrant purple. "Looking good, Suzette."

I stick my tongue out at him, which I'm sure is now some outrageous color. "You're one to talk."

We continue to eat our ice cream, laughing at each new color combination. As we near the bottom of our cones, Galileo calls out, "Don't forget, the last bite's the best."

Curious, I take the final bite of my cone. Suddenly, my hair returns to its natural color, but now it's gently floating around my head as if I'm underwater.

Throk finishes his cone as well, and his beard begins to grow at an alarming rate, quickly reaching his knees before stopping.

"Oh, that's a good look for you," I tease, reaching out to twirl a strand of his newly lengthened beard around my finger.

He captures my hand in his, sending a jolt of electricity through me. "You don't look so bad yourself, mermaid."

We thank Galileo and step back outside, the magical effects of the ice cream slowly fading. While walking, he keeps hold of my hand. "What do you think of Evershift Haven so far?"

I look up at him, taking in the genuine curiosity in his expression. "It's incredible. Overwhelming, terrifying, but also wonderful. I never imagined a place like this could exist."

He smiles. "I'm glad you're enjoying it. There's so much more I want to show you."

As we continue our tour, I hope that my car takes a very, very long time to fix because right now, there's nowhere else I'd rather be than here, exploring this magical town with Throk by my side.

After several more shops, and as the sun begins to dip low, he leads me toward the edge of town. The cobblestone streets give way to a dirt path, and soon, we're surrounded by towering trees with leaves that shimmer like gemstones in the fading light.

"Welcome to the Whispering Woods," he says with hushed reverence.

I step closer to him until our arms touch. The air here feels charged with an energy I can't quite explain. "It's beautiful," I say, tilting my head back to take in the canopy above us.

We walk deeper into the woods, and it seems strange. The leaves seem to rustle even when there's no breeze, and I swear I can hear faint whispers carried on the air. "Are the trees... talking?" I ask, my eyes wide with wonder.

Throk grins, his tusks glinting in the twilight. "They are. The trees here love to gossip. Want to hear what they're saying?"

I nod eagerly, and he guides me to a massive oak tree with gnarled branches that reach out like welcoming arms. He places his hand on the trunk and closes his eyelids, as if listening intently.

"This old fellow says he's seen many couples walk these paths over the centuries," he translates, a hint of amusement in his voice. "He thinks we make a cute pair."

Heat rises to my cheeks, and I'm grateful for the dim light that hopefully hides my blush. "Oh, really? And what do you think about that?"

He turns to face me. "I think the tree might be onto something."

My heartbeat gets erratic, and I'm lost in his gaze. For a moment, I forget about the impossibility of our situation—that he's an orc and I'm a human, and we come from completely different worlds. All I can focus on is the warmth of his presence and my pressing attraction to him.

We continue our stroll through the woods, and the whispers grow louder. Some of the trees seem to be swaying their branches toward us, as if trying to get our attention.

"What are they saying now?" I ask, curiosity getting the better of me.

Throk listens for a moment, then lets out a deep, rumbling laugh. "You might not want to know. These old trees can be quite...poetic when the mood strikes them."

"You can't leave me hanging like that." I nudge him with my elbow. "Spill it."

He obliges. "That maple over there is reciting what sounds like a sonnet about 'two hearts entwined like vines.' And the birch next to it is adding something about 'eyes that sparkle brighter than dew-kissed leaves at dawn.'"

I burst out laughing, both amused and oddly touched by the trees' romantic inclinations. "Who knew plants could be such romantics?"

"They've had centuries to perfect their craft," he says with a wink. "Though I have to admit, they're not entirely off base."

My laughter fades, replaced by a fluttering sensation in my stomach. I look up at Throk, really taking him in. His forest-green skin, the intricate darker green tribal markings on his arms, and the way his long black hair is tied back in a messy man-bun. Everything about him should seem alien, and yet... "I owe you an apology."

He tilts his head, curiosity plain on his face. "What for?"

I pause to organize my thoughts, not wanting to inadvertently insult him. "When we first met, I didn't believe you were really an orc. I thought it was all some elaborate costume or prank, but now, I can see I was wrong. You are who you say you are, and this place—Evershift Haven—is real. All of it."

His expression softens, and he takes my hand in his much larger one. "I know it's a lot to take in. I'm glad you're starting to see the truth of our world."

"It's incredible. Frightening and overwhelming at times but also magical in every sense of the word."

We stand there for a second, hands clasped and surrounded by the whispering trees. The air is thick with possibility, and I move closer to Throk, drawn by an invisible force. Suddenly, the trees around us burst into a chorus of whispers, their leaves rustling excitedly. He listens for a moment, then bursts out laughing.

"What?" I ask, both amused and slightly embarrassed. "What are they saying?"

He shakes his head, still chuckling. "Let's just say they're very invested in how this scene plays out. Apparently, we're better than their favorite soap opera."

I laugh, the tension of the moment broken. "We wouldn't want to disappoint our audience, would we?"

As soon as the words leave my mouth, I realize the insinuation. His eyes widen slightly, and he takes a small step closer. "May I kiss you?"

My heart races, and for a brief moment, all my doubts and fears come rushing back. He's an orc, and I'm a human. I barely know him. This whole situation is insane. Then I look into his eyes, warm and kind and full of genuine affection, and all those doubts melt away. I nod, not trusting my voice.

He cups my face gently with one large hand, caressing my cheek with his thumb. He leans down, and I stretch up on my tiptoes to meet him halfway. Our lips meet, and it's like nothing I've ever experienced before. His lips are softer than I expected, and there's a slight pressure from his tusks against my skin. It's foreign and familiar all at once, sending sparks of electricity through my entire body.

As we kiss, the trees around us erupt in a chorus of whispers and rustling leaves. It's as if the entire forest is cheering us on, and I smile against his lips.

When we finally pull apart, both slightly breathless, I open my eyes to find Throk gazing at me with wonder and joy. "Wow," I whisper, feeling a bit dazed.

He grins. "Wow, indeed."

We stand there for a moment, still wrapped in each other's arms, as the forest settles back into a contented hum around us. I rest my head against Throk's broad chest, listening to the steady beat of his heart. "So," I say after a while, looking up at him with a mischievous smile. "What's the verdict from our leafy audience?"

He listens for a moment, then rolls his eyes good-naturedly. "They're giving us a standing ovation. Apparently, we've just made forest history."

I laugh, feeling light and giddy. "I'd hate to disappoint them. Maybe we should give them an encore performance?"

Throk's eyes darken with desire, and he pulls me closer. "I like the way you think, Suzette."

As our lips meet again, I silently thank whatever twist of fate brought me to Evershift Haven. Surrounded by whispering trees and wrapped in Throk's strong arms, the kiss deepens, and I lose myself in the sensation. He strokes my back as I tangle my fingers in his hair, marveling at its softness.

When we finally come up for air, I'm panting slightly. He rests his forehead against mine, and his breath is warm on my face. The trees around us burst into another round of excited whispers. Leaves rain down on us like confetti, shimmering with an otherworldly light.

"I think they approve." He chuckles while brushing a leaf out of my hair.

I grin up at him, feeling happier than I have in years. "We aim to please."

Chapter 5

I SMOOTH DOWN MY DRESS, a simple black number that hugs my curves just right. My heart flutters with anticipation as I wait for Throk in the "Moonlit Inn's" lobby the next evening for our first official date. The grandfather clock in the corner ticks away, its hands moving in a mesmerizing dance.

The door swings open, and there he is. Throk fills the doorway, his broad shoulders and towering height making him an imposing figure, but his amber eyes are warm, and a smile plays on his lips. "You look beautiful."

Heat rises in my cheeks. "Thanks. You clean up pretty well yourself."

He's wearing dark jeans and a button-down shirt that stretches across his muscular chest. His long black hair is tied back in a neat bun, and his beard is freshly trimmed.

"Ready to go?" He extends his arm, and I take it, marveling at the contrast between his forest-green skin and my pale complexion.

We step outside into the cool evening air. The streets of Evershift Haven are alive with twinkling lights and the soft murmur of conversation from various magical creatures strolling about.

"Where are we going?" I ask, curiosity getting the better of me.

His lips curl into a mischievous grin. "It's a surprise, but I think you'll like it."

He leads me down winding cobblestone streets, past shops with glowing windows and bustling cafes. We turn a corner, and I gasp.

Before us stands a massive tree, its trunk wider than any I've ever seen. Lanterns hang from its branches, casting a warm, golden glow. Tables are nestled among its roots, and creatures of all shapes and sizes sit chatting and dining.

"Welcome to the Whispering Willow," Throk says, gesturing to the tree-turned-restaurant. "Best food in Evershift Haven, and the ambiance can't be beat."

A dryad with bark-like skin and leaves for hair greets us at the entrance. "Table for two?" she asks, her voice like rustling leaves.

Throk nods, and she leads us to a cozy nook formed by two massive roots. The table is made from a cross-section of the tree itself, polished to a smooth shine.

Settling in, I notice the leaves above us shifting and moving, even though there's no breeze. "Are the leaves whispering?"

Throk chuckles. "They are. The Whispering Willow loves gossip just like the other trees, and they can converse over vast distances due to their intertwined root systems. Don't worry though. She's very discreet."

A menu materializes in front of me, the words shimmering and changing as I read them. "What do you recommend?" I ask, overwhelmed by the magical options.

"The Moonlight Mushroom Risotto is excellent," he says. "And maybe we could share the Fairy Ring Appetizer?"

I nod, intrigued. When our waiter, a sprightly air spirit, arrives we place our order.

As we wait for our food, he eases forward, resting his elbows on the table. "So, Suzette, tell me more about your life in the human world. What's it like being a lawyer?"

I take a sip of the shimmering, color-changing cocktail that had appeared moments ago. "It's worse than I expected," I say with perhaps too much honesty. "Long hours and high pressure..."

Throk listens intently as I share stories of difficult cases and courtroom victories, realizing as I count them that the victories don't feel so victorious. "Once, I was going to be an attorney who made a difference. Now, I just help corporations get richer." I sigh softly and realize how long it's been since I've had a conversation like this—where I'm not constantly checking my phone or thinking about the next deadline. It gives me too much time to think and start to question my life choices.

Our appetizer arrives—a literal fairy ring of tiny, glowing mushrooms. We sample them, and bursts of flavor explode on my tongue—sweet, savory, and utterly otherworldly.

"What about you?" I ask, popping another mushroom into my mouth. "How did you end up running a magical auto shop?"

He grins. "I've always been fascinated by human technology. As a kid, I'd sneak to the edge of Evershift Haven, watching the cars go by on the highway. One day, an old human mechanic caught me. Instead of shooing me away, he started teaching me about human engines."

He pauses as our main courses arrive. My risotto glows softly in the dim light, tiny stars seeming to swirl within the creamy rice.

"I was hooked," he says, cutting into his Chimera Steak, which seems to be three different types of meat in one. "When I was old enough, I started apprenticing at 'Mystical Motors' to learn about magical engines and naturally blended the two together to become a unique mechanic in either world. When the old owner retired, he asked if I wanted to take over."

While we eat, he shares tales of the strangest car problems he's encountered—from a dragon that had made a nest in someone's engine to a curse that caused a car to only drive in reverse.

Before I know it, our plates are empty, and the sky has darkened to a deep indigo. Throk pays the bill with what looks like glowing gemstones, and we step back out into the night.

"Ready for part two of our evening?" he asks, a twinkle in his eye.

I raise an eyebrow. "There's more?"

He nods, taking my hand. The warmth of his skin sends a pleasant tingle up my arm. "I promised to show you what's really going on with your car, remember?"

We walk hand in hand through the quiet streets of Evershift Haven. The town seems different at night—more mysterious and even more magical. I swear I can hear the faint tinkling of fairy laughter.

As we approach "Mystical Motors," there's a soft glow emanating from within. Throk pulls out a key that seems to be made of pure light and unlocks the door.

"Welcome to my world," he says, ushering me inside.

The garage is unlike anything I've ever seen. Tools float in mid-air, arranging and rearranging themselves. A soft humming fills the air, punctuated by occasional clangs and whirs, and there, in the center of it all, is my car.

But it's not quite how I remember it. The pink metal seems to shimmer and shift, and there's an aura of...something around it. Energy? Magic? "What's happened to Vivi?" As I ask that, the headlights, complete with lashes, turn my direction as if she's looking at me. It's unnerving but kind of cool.

Throk leads me closer. "Watch this," he says, placing his hand on the hood.

Instantly, the car comes to life—not starting up, but literally coming alive. The headlights blink like eyes, and the grill seems to form a mouth.

I stumble back, shocked. "What... how...?"

Throk grins. "Your car absorbed some wild magic when it crossed into Evershift Haven. It's become semi-sentient."

As if to prove his point, Vivi lets out a honk that sounds suspiciously like a greeting.

"Is this...permanent?" I ask, cautiously approaching the vehicle.

Throk shakes his head. "No, it'll fade once we get the right parts, and I can realign its magical field before you drive away. Once you're out of Evershift Haven, it'll be back to normal, but for now..." He pats the hood affectionately. "You've got yourself a pretty unique ride."

I reach out, hesitantly touching the warm metal. The car shudders slightly under my hand, almost like a cat purring.

"This is incredible," I say, looking up at Throk. His face is illuminated by the soft glow of the floating tools. "Hello, Vivi," I say politely.

The car honks its horn, and the grill forms a smile.

He steps closer, and I'm suddenly very aware of how little space there is between us. "I know this must all be overwhelming for you, but I want you to know I'm glad your car broke down here. I'm glad I got to meet you."

My heart races. I'm a rational person, a lawyer who deals in facts and evidence, but here, in this magical garage, with Throk, rationality seems less important.

I stand on my tiptoes, bringing my face closer to his. "I'm glad too," I whisper.

He leans down, his lips meeting mine in a kiss that sends sparks through my entire body—literal sparks, as the tools around us start to spin and dance in response to our emotions.

When we break apart, both slightly breathless, I laugh. "Is it always going to be like this?" I ask, gesturing to the whirlwind of magical activity around us.

Throk grins, pulling me closer. "Undoubtedly."

I gaze up at him, heart pounding as our gazes lock. The magical whirlwind around us settles, leaving a charged silence.

He clears his throat. "Would you like to see my place upstairs? I could show you my collection of human world tools."

A thrill runs through me at the invitation. There's only one tool I really want to see right now though. "I'd love to."

He takes my hand, leading me to a narrow staircase hidden behind a rack of enchanted wrenches. We climb, and the wood creaks beneath our feet, each step bringing us closer to his private domain.

At the top, he pushes open a heavy oak door. "Welcome to my humble abode."

I step inside and take in the space. It's a cozy loft, filled with an eclectic mix of magical artifacts and mundane human objects. A worn leather couch sits beside a bookshelf crammed with tomes on both mechanics and spellcraft. On the far wall, a workbench is covered in half-finished projects with gears and crystals intermingling.

"This is amazing." I run my fingers along the spines of his books. "You really do love blending magic and technology."

He moves closer, his presence warm at my back. "It's my passion. I've always been fascinated by how things work, whether they're powered by electricity or arcane energy."

I turn to face him, suddenly very aware of how close we are. His expression is intense, filled with a mixture of desire and something deeper—a genuine interest that makes my breath catch.

"Can I show you something?" he asks, his voice low.

I nod, not trusting myself to speak.

He leads me to the workbench, picking up what looks like an ordinary wrench. "Watch this."

As he speaks, the wrench begins to glow softly. Its metal form shifts and changes, elongating into a delicate silver wand. "It's a shapeshifting tool. Useful for both magical and mechanical work."

I reach out, hesitantly touching the wand. A spark of energy dances across my fingertips. "It's incredible."

"Like you," he says softly.

I look up, meeting his gaze. The air between us crackles with tension. Without thinking, I sway closer, pressing my lips to his.

Throk responds immediately, wrapping his strong arms around me. His lips are surprisingly soft against mine, and I melt into the kiss. I explore the broad expanse of his chest, marveling at the firm muscles beneath his shirt.

As the kiss deepens, I become acutely aware of our physical differences. He towers over me, his body solid and powerful. His skin is warm, with a slight roughness that makes my panties damp. The small tusks that protrude from his lower lip add an exotic thrill to each caress.

We break apart, both breathing heavily. His eyes are dark with desire. "Suzette, I want you. Is that what you want too?"

In response, I pull him down for another kiss. This time, there's no hesitation. Throk lifts me effortlessly, carrying me to a large bed in the corner of the loft. He lays me down gently, covering me with his massive form.

I run my hands along his arms, feeling the intricate patterns of his tribal markings. They seem to pulse with energy beneath my touch. "These are beautiful."

Throk smiles, a flash of white teeth against his green skin. "They're more than decorative. Each marking represents a different magical skill or achievement."

"Show me."

He takes my hand, guiding it to a swirling pattern on his bicep. As I trace the design, a warm glow emanates from the marking. Suddenly, the air around us fills with tiny, shimmering lights, like a personal galaxy.

I gasp in wonder. "It's like starlight."

"It's a spell for illumination. Useful in the garage, but also rather romantic, don't you think?"

In the soft, magical light, Throk's features are even more striking. I reach up, running my fingers through his locks.

Our kisses grow more heated, hands exploring with increasing urgency. Throk's fingers are surprisingly dexterous as they work the buttons of my dress. I tug at his shirt, eager to see more of his muscular green body.

As our clothes fall away, I'm struck by the beauty of our contrasts. My pale skin against his forest green, and his substantial frame dwarfing my more petite figure. Somehow, we fit together perfectly.

Throk's touch is gentle despite his strength, and every caress sends sparks of pleasure through me. I explore his body with equal fervor, tracing the lines of his muscles and discovering sensitive spots that make him groan.

I can't believe this is happening. His hands are on me, his lips pressed against mine, and I'm melting into him. His skin is warm and rough in contrast to my own softness. I run my fingers through his long black hair, loosing his man-bun, and pulling him closer as our kiss deepens.

He trails kisses down my neck. I gasp as his teeth graze my collarbone, the sensation both painful and pleasurable. I arch my back, pressing myself against him, wanting more.

Throk's hands roam my body, exploring every curve and contour. He cups my breasts, teasing my nipples through the thin fabric of my bra, since my dress is currently on the floor. I moan, my hips bucking against him.

He pulls back, looking into my eyes. "Are you sure about this?" he asks.

I nod, my breath coming in short gasps. "Yes, I want this. I want you."

Throk smiles, a wicked gleam in his amber eyes. He stands up, towering over me. He slowly undresses, revealing his muscular body. His cock is huge—much larger than any human's, and ridged with veins. A small barb protrudes from the head, and I wonder what it feels like.

Throk notices my wide-eyed gaze and chuckles. "Don't worry. It won't hurt. It's designed to enhance your pleasure."

He kneels down in front of me, pushing panties to my feet, and I step out of them. I'm exposed, vulnerable, but I trust him. Throk kisses my thighs, his lips soft and gentle. He moves higher, his breath hot against my skin.

I gasp as his tongue flicks against my clit. He licks and sucks, teasing me until I'm writhing beneath him. I grab onto his hair, pulling him closer as I grind against my pussy against his face. His fingers join the party, sliding easily inside me. I'm wet and ready for him, my body aching for release. He curls his fingers, hitting that sweet spot inside me, and I cry out, my orgasm like an impending tidal wave.

Throk doesn't let up, working his tongue and fingers in tandem. I come hard, my body shaking as waves of pleasure wash over me. Once I'm done trembling, and he's coaxed all the pleasure from me with several aftershocks fueled by his textured tongue, he pulls back with a satisfied grin on his face.

"Are you ready for me?" he asks, his voice rough with desire.

I nod, legs still trembling. If I weren't sitting on the bed, I'd be on the floor in a heap like my dress. Throk positions his cock at my pussy, pressing the head against my opening. He's so much bigger than any human man, and I have a moment of hesitation.

Before I can even really think about it, let alone verbalize it, he's pushing inside me, inch by inch. It's a tight fit, but he's patient and gentle. I feel stretched and overly full, but it's not painful. It's...amazing.

He starts to move, thrusting his hips slowly. Each stroke sends shockwaves of pleasure through my body. I wrap my legs around him, pulling him closer.

He leans down, capturing my lips in a searing kiss. Our tongues dance together as he fucks me, his cock hitting all the right spots. That strange barb nestles against my clit, quietly humming with its own vibration as he plunges in and out of me, stimulating my clit no matter which way he's moving. I moan into his mouth, digging my nails into his back.

He quickens his pace, and his thrusts becoming more disjointed. The faster he goes, the more his barb catches on my inner walls, anchoring us together. It's an odd sensation, but not unpleasant. In fact, it heightens my pleasure, making me feel even more connected to him.

I come again, convulsing as I cry out his name. He follows shortly after, his cock pulsing inside me as he fills me with his seed. We stay like that for a moment, our bodies entwined, our breathing ragged.

Throk pulls out, and his cock is still semi-hard. He collapses beside me, his chest heaving. I curl up against him, my head resting on his shoulder as his release floods out of me before slowing to a trickle. He must have a prodigious amount of cum. "That was incredible," I say breathlessly.

Throk chuckles. "I aim to please."

We lie there in silence, our bodies still humming with pleasure. I can't believe I just had sex with an orc, but I don't regret it. Throk is kind, gentle, and incredibly sexy. I could get used to this.

His fingers trace patterns on my skin, making me shiver with desire that's rising again already. "What are you thinking about?"

I smile. "Just how lucky I am to have met you."

He down to kiss me. "The feeling is mutual, Suzette."

We kiss lazily, our bodies still entwined. I don't know what the future holds, but for now, I'm content to be here with Throk, exploring this strange and wonderful new world. "I was also thinking..."

"Hmm?"

"Maybe we could do that again. Whenever you're ready, I mean." I rub my thigh against his cock, which is suddenly fully erect again.

His response is somewhere between a laugh and a growl as he repositions me and slides inside my pussy again seconds later. It's going to be a long, wonderful night.

Chapter 6

I WAKE TO A GENTLE knock on my door. Blinking away sleep, I sit up in the plush bed at the "Moonlit Inn," briefly forgetting how I got there before recalling Throk had brought me back in the wee hours, so I'd have my new clothes and toiletries at my disposal. Sunlight streams through the curtains, letting me know it's definitely morning, though I could sleep several more hours after last night's...exercise.

"Come in," I say, running a hand through my tangled hair before testing my breath. Not too bad. Maybe magical food reduces halitosis.

The door opens, and Crystal glides in, her auburn locks cascading over her shoulders. She's almost vibrating with excitement. "Good morning, Suzette. I hope I didn't wake you too early."

I shake my head. "Not at all. What's up?"

She perches on the edge of my bed, her gothic-inspired dress rustling softly, and I catch a hint of fangs when she talks, making me suspect my hosts are vampires, but I don't know how to ask. I'm not afraid they'll suck my blood, so I don't bother.

"I have a favor to ask. We're a bit shorthanded for the Monster Mash festival preparations. Would you be willing to lend a hand?"

The Monster Mash festival. Right. Another reminder that I'm stuck in this bizarre town where supernatural creatures are apparently real, but after my date with Throk last night, I'm finding it harder to deny—or resist—the magic around me. "Sure," I say, surprising myself with my eagerness. "What do you need help with?"

Her smile widens. Yes, definitely fangs. "Wonderful. We're enchanting jack-o'-lanterns to hover along the streets. It's quite a sight when it's done."

I raise an eyebrow. "Enchanting jack-o'-lanterns? How exactly does that work?"

She winks at me. "You'll see. Why don't you get dressed and meet me downstairs in about thirty minutes? We'll have breakfast first."

After Crystal leaves, I hop out of bed and head to the bathroom. As I brush my teeth, I stare at my reflection in the mirror. The gold flecks in my brown eyes seem brighter somehow, as if the magic of Evershift Haven is seeping into me.

Downstairs, I find Crystal and Etienne in the dining room. The smell of fresh coffee and warm pastries fills the air. Etienne, impeccable as always in his vintage suit, pours me a cup of coffee.

"Good morning, Suzette," he says happily, and again, I see some fang. "I hear you've volunteered to help with the festival preparations."

I nod, taking a sip of the rich, dark coffee. "It seemed like the least I could do, considering how welcoming you've all been."

Crystal beams at me. "We're so glad you're embracing the spirit of Evershift Haven."

While we eat breakfast, Crystal explains more about the Monster Mash festival. It's one of the town's biggest celebrations that is close to, but not on, human Halloween. It's a time when the veil between the human world and the supernatural realm is at its thinnest.

"It's like Halloween on steroids," says Etienne with a chuckle.

After breakfast, we head out to the town square. The air is crisp and cool, carrying the scent of autumn leaves and spices. In the center of the square, a group of people—or rather, creatures—are gathered around a pile of pumpkins.

I sigh like a lovestruck teen when I spot Throk among them. He towers over the others, his green skin glistening in the morning sun. When he sees me, he lights up, and he waves at me.

"Suzette?" he calls out, striding toward us. "You're helping with the preparations?"

I nod, suddenly feeling a bit shy. "Crystal asked if I could lend a hand."

He grins. "Great. I'm here to help too. Shall we get started?"

Crystal leads us to the pile of pumpkins. Up close, I can see that they're not ordinary pumpkins. Their surfaces shimmer with an otherworldly glow, and their shapes are more varied and fantastical than any jack-o'-lanterns I've seen before.

"Attention, everyone," says Crystal, clapping her hands loudly. "Let's begin the enchantment process. For our newcomers," She winks at me, "Watch closely and try to follow along."

I watch while she picks up a pumpkin and places her hands on either side of it. She closes her eyes, and a soft violet light emanates from her palms. The pumpkin begins to rise slowly from her hands, hovering a few inches above them.

"The key is to focus your energy into the pumpkin," she says, her eyelids still closed. "Visualize it floating, weightless and free. The spell Grizelda cast will do the rest. You don't even need your own magic if you haven't found it yet." She opens her eyes and winks at me again.

Around me, others begin to follow suit. I see a werewolf lifting a wolf-shaped pumpkin, its eyes glowing an eerie yellow. A fairy flutters around a tiny, delicate pumpkin, sprinkling it with what looks like pixie dust.

Throk nudges me gently. "Want to try?"

I nod, still a bit dazed. "I'm not sure I can do it though. I'm not magical."

He chuckles. "Everyone has a bit of magic in them. You just need to believe in it." Throk picks up a pumpkin and holds it out to me. It's smaller than the others, with intricate swirling patterns carved into its surface.

I take it from him, surprised by its lightness.

"Close your eyes. Feel the pumpkin in your hands. Imagine it's filled with helium, light as a balloon."

I do as he says, feeling a bit foolish, but as I concentrate, I start to feel a tingling sensation in my palms. It spreads up my arms, warm and pulsing.

"That's it," he encourages. "Slowly lift your hands away from the pumpkin."

Taking a deep breath, I raise my hands. For a moment, nothing happens. Then the pumpkin leaves my palms. I open my eyelids to see it floating a few inches above my hands, surrounded by a faint golden glow. "I did it." I laugh in disbelief.

Throk beams at me, his pride evident. "See? I told you you had magic in you."

We spend the next few hours enchanting pumpkins. With each one, it gets a little easier. I'm enjoying the process, impressed at the way the jack-o'-lanterns bob and weave in the air once enchanted.

As we work, I chat with some of the other volunteers. There's Willow the dryad, whom I met on my first day in town, and Galileo, the frost giant who owns the ice cream parlor. He's fashioning jack-o'-lanterns that emit a cool mist.

"So, Suzette," Willow says while we work side by side, "How are you finding Evershift Haven so far?"

I pause, considering my answer. "It's not what I expected, but in a good way, I think."

Willow smiles, her leaf-green eyes twinkling. "It has a way of growing on you, doesn't it? I remember when I first arrived here, centuries ago. I was just a sapling then, barely more than a twig."

"Centuries?" I ask, my eyes widening. "How old are you?"

She laughs, the sound like rustling leaves. "Oh, it's impolite to ask a lady her age, but let's just say I've seen many Monster Mash festivals come and go."

As we continue enchanting pumpkins, a commotion erupts from the far side of the town square. I turn to see Grizelda, her wild mane of silver-streaked purple hair even more disheveled than usual, engaged in a heated argument with Atlas. Their voices carry across the square, drawing curious glances from the other volunteers.

"Atlas, darling, we can't line every surface of our home with cushioning charms." Grizelda waves her hands dramatically. "Our child needs to learn about the world, bumps and all."

Atlas, his massive frame towering over Grizelda, crosses his arms. "But what if the little one falls? Or touches something sharp? We need to be prepared for every possibility."

"Every possibility?" Grizelda scoffs. "Next you'll want to bubble-wrap the entire town."

Their bickering continues, growing more animated by the second. I edge toward Throk, raising an eyebrow. "What's that all about?"

Throk chuckles. "Grizelda and Atlas are expecting their first child. They've been arguing about baby-proofing their home for weeks now."

"A baby?" I ask, surprised. "I didn't even know that was possible between... well..."

"A witch and a troll?" he finishes for me. "In Evershift Haven, anything's possible. Though I suspect their child will be quite the handful."

Grizelda throws up her hands in exasperation. A burst of sparks shoots from her fingertips, cascading over the pile of enchanted pumpkins we've been working on all morning. For a moment, nothing happens.

Then chaos erupts.

The pumpkins begin to twitch and shake, their carved faces contorting into expressions of mischief and glee. One by one, they start to rise into the air, no longer gently floating but zooming about with alarming speed.

"Oh, no," Crystal mutters beside me. "Grizelda's accidentally animated them."

Before I can ask what that means, a nearby pumpkin swoops down, its jagged mouth snapping at my hair. I duck just in time, feeling the rush of air as it passes overhead.

"Watch out," shouts Throk, pulling me close as another pumpkin dives toward us.

All around the square, turmoil reigns. The enchanted pumpkins, now fully alive and apparently with minds of their own, wreak havoc. They zoom through the air, knocking over decorations and chasing terrified townsfolk.

I watch in disbelief as a group of jack-o'-lanterns corner a startled werewolf, their carved grins seeming more menacing by the second. Another pumpkin, shaped like a bat, flaps its leafy wings and dive-bombs a group of pixies, scattering them in a shower of glitter.

"We need to do something," I shout over the screams and maniacal pumpkin cackles.

Throk nods. "We need to round them up before they spread to the rest of town."

As if on cue, a particularly large pumpkin with a wicked grin zooms past us, heading straight for Main Street. Throk takes off after it, his long strides eating up the ground. Without thinking, I follow him.

We race down the street, dodging pedestrians and airborne gourds alike. Ahead of us, the rogue pumpkin terrorizes a group of ghosts outside the "Spellbound Cinema," cackling as it passes right through their translucent forms.

"How do we stop it?" I'm panting and struggling to keep up with Throk's pace.

He glances back at me, his expression grim. "We need to catch it and dispel the animation charm, but be careful—their bites can be nasty."

As if to prove his point, a nearby pumpkin lunges at a passing fairy, its teeth sinking into her gossamer wing. The fairy shrieks, more in indignation than pain, and swats at the pumpkin with her wand.

We continue our chase, weaving through the streets of Evershift Haven. The town, usually so charming and amazing, now seems like a Halloween nightmare come to life. Jack-o'-lanterns dart in and out of shops, causing havoc wherever they go. One smashes through the window of "The Enchanted Espresso," sending patrons scrambling for cover.

"There." Throk points ahead. Our target pumpkin has paused in its rampage, hovering ominously above the fountain in Mystic Meadows.

We approach cautiously, trying not to startle it. The pumpkin turns, its carved eyes seeming to narrow as it spots us. For a moment, we stand in a tense standoff.

With a wicked cackle, the pumpkin dives straight for us.

Throk reacts instantly, reaching with his large hands to grab it, but the pumpkin is quicker, slipping through his fingers and zooming around his head. It lets out another chortle, almost as if it's taunting us.

"We need to trap it somehow," I shout, ducking as the pumpkin makes another pass at us.

He nods, scanning our surroundings. Suddenly, he grins. "The fountain. If we can get it in the water, it'll slow it down."

It's a crazy plan, but it's all we've got. I nod, and we begin to maneuver ourselves, trying to herd the pumpkin toward the fountain. It darts and weaves, always just out of reach. Just as I think we've got it cornered, the pumpkin makes a sudden dive. I lunge forward, arms outstretched, but my foot catches on the edge of the fountain. I stumble, losing my balance.

Time seems to slow down as I fall forward, bracing myself for the impact with the water, but instead of a splash, strong arms wrap around me, pulling me back. Throk steadies me, his solid presence a comfort amidst the chaos.

"Are you okay?"

I nod, catching my breath. "Thanks to you."

Our moment is interrupted by a splash. We look up to see the pumpkin floating in the fountain, its movements sluggish in the water. Without hesitation, he reaches in and grabs it, holding it firmly despite its squirming.

As he's lifting it out, he gets close to me. I yelp when the gourd wiggles enough to bite my hand. "Little bugger." I glare at it as it grins at me without repentance. "Now what?"

"Let's get back to the square. I'm sure there's a plan in the works already."

I suck on my stinging finger and trade glares with the evil little pumpkin while we walk back toward the site of calamity once more.

Chapter 7

WE RUSH BACK TO THE town square. The chaos of animated pumpkins greets us—orange blurs zipping through the air, cackling with mischievous glee. Grizelda stands in the center of it all, crackling with magical energy.

"Ah, there you two are." She waves us over. "I've got a plan to wrangle these rascals." As she speaks, she waves her hand, and the evil pumpkin that bit me becomes harmless once more, floating gently as it was designed to do as Throk releases it.

I dodge a low-flying jack-o'-lantern. "What's the plan?"

She produces a shimmering net from thin air. "These enchanted nets will nullify the animation spell, but we'll need precise timing and teamwork to catch those slippery squashes."

Atlas lumbers up, his massive frame dwarfing everyone around him. "I'll take point. Follow my lead, folks."

The townsfolk gather around, a motley crew of humans, magical creatures, and everything in between. I grab a net, the gossamer material tingling against my skin.

"Ready?" shouts Atlas. "Let's go pumpkin hunting."

We spread out across the square. I stick close to Throk, drawing comfort from his solid presence. A jack-o'-lantern swoops down, its carved grin leering at us.

"Now." Atlas roars.

I swing my net in unison with Throk. The pumpkin tries to dodge, but we anticipate its move. The net envelops it, and instantly, the jack-o'-lantern goes still.

"We got one." I grin at Throk.

He pats my shoulder. "Nice teamwork, Suzette."

All around us, similar scenes play out. Grizelda pirouettes gracefully, snagging three pumpkins at once. Atlas uses his height advantage to pluck them right out of the air. Even Etienne and Crystal join in, their vampire speed giving them an edge.

As we work, I can't stop laughing. The absurdity of the situation hits me—here I am, a corporate lawyer, chasing magical pumpkins with an orc, and I'm having the time of my life.

A particularly wily jack-o'-lantern evades capture, cackling as it zooms between buildings. "I've got this one," I shout, breaking into a run.

The pumpkin leads me on a merry chase through Evershift Haven. I duck under floating shop signs, weave through a group of startled gnomes, and leap over a snoozing troll. Finally, I corner it in a dead-end alley.

"Gotcha now." I'm panting as I raise my net.

The jack-o'-lantern's eyes narrow. Suddenly, it spits a glob of pumpkin guts at me. I yelp, diving to the side. The gooey mess splats against the wall behind me.

"Oh, it's on now," I say with a growl. I feint left, then lunge right. The pumpkin falls for it, and I bring my net down with a triumphant, "Ha."

Cradling my captured quarry, I jog back to the town square. The chaos has died down, with most of the animated pumpkins now safely contained.

Throk spots me and rushes over. "Are you okay? You disappeared for a while there."

I hold up my prize. "Just had to teach this little troublemaker a lesson."

He chuckles, his deep laugh rumbling through me. "That's my girl."

Grizelda approaches, clapping her hands. "Well done, everyone. I think we've got them all." She looks at my pumpkin. "Ooh, that's a feisty one. Good catch, dear."

As the townspeople gather, a celebratory mood settles over us. Atlas starts stacking the captured pumpkins into a massive pyramid, much to everyone's delight.

As the excitement of our pumpkin-catching adventure dies down, I notice a sharp sting on my finger. Looking down, I see a small, jagged cut where the feisty jack-o'-lantern bit me earlier. It's not deep, but it tingles in an odd way.

Grizelda tuts as she spots the injury. "Oh, dear, let me see that." She gently takes my hand, examining the bite with a frown. "Hmm, this won't do at all."

"It's just a small cut," I say, trying to downplay her concern. "I'm sure it'll be fine."

Grizelda shakes her head. "My dear, this is no ordinary cut. That pumpkin was enchanted, and its bite carries magic. If we don't act quickly, you might find yourself turning into a jack-o'-lantern at the next full moon."

I laugh nervously, searching her face for any sign that she's joking. Her expression remains deadly serious. "What? People don't just turn into pumpkins."

"In Evershift Haven, anything is possible," says Throk with concern.

She nods emphatically. "Exactly, so hold still. I need to perform a quick spell to neutralize the magic before it takes root."

Part of me wants to protest, to insist that this is all some elaborate prank, but after everything I've seen in this strange town, I can't dismiss the possibility outright. With a resigned sigh, I hold out my hand. "Okay, do what you need to do."

Grizelda's eyes light up, quite literally. A soft purple glow emanates from her irises as she begins to chant in a language I don't recognize. The air around us seems to thicken, charged with an unseen energy that makes the hairs on my arms stand on end.

As she speaks, Grizelda traces intricate patterns in the air above my injured finger. Sparks of golden light trail from her fingertips, weaving a complex web of shimmering magic. The tingling in my cut intensifies before fading to a cool, soothing sensation. With a final flourish, she snaps her fingers, and the golden web collapses inward, sinking into my skin with a flash. I gasp, more from surprise than pain.

"There we go." She beams, looking quite pleased with herself. "That should do the trick. How does it feel?"

I flex my finger experimentally. The cut has already begun to heal, the edges knitting together before my eyes. "It feels good actually. Thank you."

"Wonderful. No need to worry about sprouting vines or turning orange now—though I must say, you would have made a rather fetching jack-o'-lantern."

I laugh, shaking my head at the absurdity of it all. "I think I'll stick to being human, thanks."

As the crowd begins to disperse, Throk steps closer. "That was quite an adventure. You handled yourself well out there."

I smile up at him, feeling a flutter in my stomach that has nothing to do with magical pumpkin bites. "Thanks. I have to admit, it was kind of fun."

His eyes crinkle at the corners as he grins. "I'm glad you enjoyed it. Listen, I was wondering..." He pauses, looking uncharacteristically nervous. "Would you like to come back to my place? Maybe we could have dinner?"

"I'd love to," I hear myself saying before I can overthink it. I hope for a repeat of last night.

His tusks seem prominent as his grin widens. "Great. Shall we?"

We start walking toward Throk's home as I ponder how quickly my life has changed. Just days ago, I was a corporate lawyer focused on nothing but my career. Now, I'm strolling through a magical town with an orc, having just helped capture enchanted pumpkins. When was the last time I felt this happy or relaxed in Chicago?

I follow Throk up the narrow staircase to his apartment above "Mystical Motors." The familiar scent of motor oil and magical herbs wafts through the air, making me smile. It's amazing how quickly this place has become familiar to me.

"Make yourself at home," he says, gesturing to the cozy living room. "I'll get started on dinner."

"Need any help?" I ask, peeking into the kitchen.

Throk grins, his tusks glinting in the warm light. "Sure, if you don't mind washing some vegetables."

I join him in the kitchen, marveling at the array of ingredients spread across the counter. Some I recognize while others are completely alien to me. Throk hands me a colander filled with what look like normal carrots, but they're a vibrant purple color.

"Just give those a rinse. The sink's enchanted—it'll clean them thoroughly without washing away their magical properties."

I turn on the tap, watching in fascination as the water sparkles and shimmers, enveloping the carrots in a gentle glow. "What are we making?"

"Shimmerleaf stew." He expertly dices some iridescent mushrooms. "It's an old orc recipe, but I've added my own twist."

As I wash the vegetables, he shares stories of his childhood in Evershift Haven. He tells me about his first attempts at cooking, which resulted in a small magical explosion that turned his entire family's skin blue for a week.

"My mom was furious." He chuckles, stirring a pot of simmering broth. "My dad thought it was hilarious. He kept joking that I'd finally brought out our 'true orc color.'"

I laugh, imagining a young Throk with bright blue skin. "Did you always want to be a mechanic?"

He shakes his head. "Not always. When I was little, I dreamed of being an explorer, venturing beyond the borders of Evershift Haven to see the human world, but as I grew older, I realized my passion was in understanding how things work, whether they're magical or mechanical."

He hands me an enchanted knife, its blade glowing with a soft blue light. "This will do the chopping for you. Just guide it gently."

I take the knife, marveling at how it seems to anticipate my movements. With barely any effort, I'm slicing through the purple carrots and other mysterious vegetables.

We work side by side, and the kitchen fills with tantalizing aromas. The stew bubbles merrily in its pot, occasionally letting out little musical notes that sound like tiny wind chimes.

"So," he says, a hint of nervousness in his voice, "What do you think of Evershift Haven so far? I know it must be a lot to take in."

I pause, considering my answer. "It's incredible. Overwhelming at times, but in the best possible way. I never imagined a place like this could exist."

He nods. "I'm glad you're enjoying it. I was worried you might want to leave as soon as your car was fixed."

The thought of leaving sends an unexpected pang through my chest. "I... I don't know what I'm going to do when my car's ready. Part of me knows I should get back to my job, but another part..."

"Wants to stay?" he asks softly.

I nod, unable to meet his gaze. "Is that crazy? I barely know this place, or you, but..."

He sets down his spoon and turns to fully face me. "It's not crazy at all. Magic has a way of showing us what we truly want, even if we didn't know we wanted it."

The intensity in his expression makes me hold my breath for a tick. We're standing so close now, the heat from his body enveloping me. The knife in my hand continues chopping on its own, forgotten. "Throk, I—"

A sudden hiss from the stove breaks the moment. We both turn to see the pot of stew trying to float away, little wisps of steam propelling it upwards.

"Oops." Throk lunges for the pot, grabbing it just before it can escape. "Looks like I added a bit too much levitation essence. Here, help me weigh it down."

We scramble to find heavy objects to place on the lid, laughing as the pot continues to struggle against our efforts. By the time we've got it under control, we're both breathless and grinning.

"I think dinner's ready. Shall we?"

We carry the dishes to his small dining table, which is actually a repurposed gear from some enormous machine. The stew shimmers in the bowls, tiny galaxies swirling in its depths.

"It's beautiful," I say, lifting a spoonful to my lips.

The flavor explodes across my tongue—rich and savory, with hints of spices I've never tasted before. Each bite seems to dance with a different sensation—warmth spreading through my body, a tingling on my skin, and even a momentary feeling of weightlessness.

"This is amazing," I say between bites. "I've never had anything like it."

Throk beams with pride. "I'm glad you like it. It's a special recipe, meant to be shared with someone important."

Looking at him across the table, I feel a rush of warmth that has nothing to do with the stew. We eat in comfortable silence for a while, enjoying the meal and each other's company.

As we finish, he clears his throat. "There's something I want to ask you."

I arch a brow. "Yes?"

"Would you...like to stay here? In Evershift Haven, I mean. Not necessarily with me, unless you wanted to, of course, but—"

I cut off his rambling with a gentle touch on his hand. "Throk, are you asking me to move here?"

He nods, his ears turning a telling shade of bright green. "I know it's a lot to ask. You have a life outside of here, and a career, but I feel like you belong here. With us. With...me."

The rational part of my brain wants to protest. I have responsibilities, a job, and a whole life I'd be leaving behind, but as I look into Throk's earnest face, I realize something. For the first time in years, I feel truly alive. Evershift Haven, with all its magic and wonder, has awakened something in me I didn't even know was sleeping.

I take a moment to process Throk's words. The idea of staying in Evershift Haven with him is both exhilarating and terrifying. I can't deny the connection I feel but it's a huge decision. "I'll think about it," I say finally. "I need some time to process everything."

He nods. "Of course. I didn't mean to pressure you."

The tension between us shifts, becoming charged with a different kind of energy. I lean forward, brushing my lips against his in a soft kiss. He responds eagerly, wrapping his arms around me as he deepens the kiss.

We move to his bedroom, and this night is even better than last night. When I come, I see literal stars above me on the ceiling, like tiny galaxies dying and bursting back into life. We remain like that for a while, our breathing ragged and heavy. I snuggle closer to him, my heart full of contentment.

As we bask in the afterglow of our lovemaking, I'm grateful for the strange twist of fate that brought me to Evershift Haven. I close my eyes, smiling as I drift off to sleep. My dreams are filled with visions of a bright and happy future. In sleep, it doesn't seem impossible at all.

Chapter 8

THE TOWN SQUARE BUSTLES with activity as I step into the heart of the Monster Mash festival. Colorful banners flutter overhead, proclaiming contests and games in whimsical lettering. The air crackles with excitement and magic.

"Suzette. Over here." Throk's deep voice carries over the crowd. I spot him waving near a booth festooned with brightly colored broomsticks.

I weave through the throng, dodging a group of cackling witches and sidestepping a lumbering golem. "What's all this?"

Throk grins, his tusks gleaming. "Broomstick racing. Care to give it a go?"

I eye the brooms skeptically. "I've never flown before."

"No time like the present," he says, plucking a sleek silver broom from the rack. "This one's got good balance for beginners."

Before I can protest, a cheerful fairy in a referee's uniform flits over. "New racer? Wonderful. The novice heat starts in five minutes. Here's your number."

She pins a "42" to my shirt and zooms off, leaving me clutching the broom. "Throk, I don't know about this..."

He places a reassuring hand on my shoulder. "You'll do great. Just imagine it's like riding a bike...that flies."

"Right. Piece of cake," I mutter.

The fairy's whistle pierces the air. "Novice racers to the starting line."

I join a nervous-looking group at the edge of the square. My fellow racers include a young werewolf, a timid ghost, and what appears to be a talking houseplant.

"Mount your brooms," calls the fairy.

I straddle the broom, feeling ridiculous. The silver handle vibrates slightly beneath my fingers.

"On your mark... get set... FLY."

To my astonishment, the broom lifts off the ground. I let out a startled yelp when we rise higher, my knuckles white on the handle.

"Lean forward to go faster," he shouts from below.

Instinctively, I shift my weight. The broom surges ahead, whipping wind through my hair. I laugh while weaving around a floating pumpkin obstacle.

The ghost racer passes through a chimney, taking a shortcut. The werewolf howls as he narrowly avoids a flock of bats. I'm gaining on the houseplant, its leaves fluttering wildly. Approaching the final turn, I spot the finish line and flatten myself against the broom handle, urging it faster.

The plant and I are neck and neck. With a final burst of speed, I cross the line a leaf's breadth ahead.

Cheers erupt from the crowd as I touch down, legs wobbling. Throk sweeps me into a bone-crushing hug. "You were amazing."

I'm grinning so hard my cheeks hurt. "That was incredible. When can I go again?"

The fairy referee approaches, a bronze medal in her hands. "Congratulations on third place. Not bad for your first flight."

Throk pulls me aside. "Congratulations. You're a natural at this magic stuff."

I laugh, still buzzing from the excitement. "I can't believe it. Is it always like this here?"

"Oh, this is nothing." Throk grins. "Wanna take a magic carpet ride?"

"You're joking?"

His grin widens. "Not at all. I'll show you."

He takes my hand and leads me away from the bustling festival. We wind through Evershift Haven's twisting streets as the sounds of celebration fade behind us.

"Where are we going?" I ask, curiosity getting the better of me.

"You'll see," he says with a wink.

We arrive at a small shop tucked between two larger buildings. A faded sign above the door reads "Whisper's Woven Wonders." Throk knocks three times in a distinct pattern.

The door creaks open, revealing a wizened old woman with silver hair that seems to float around her head like a cloud. Her eyes, a startling shade of violet, twinkle as she looks us over.

"Ah, Throk. And you must be Suzette. I've been expecting you." She steps aside, gesturing for us to enter.

I shoot Throk a questioning look, but he just shrugs and gently nudges me forward.

The interior of the shop is a riot of color and texture. Carpets of every size and pattern hang from the walls and ceiling, creating a maze of fabric.

"Madam Whisper." He bows slightly. "We were hoping to borrow one of your special carpets for the evening."

The old woman beams. "Of course, of course. I have just the thing." She disappears behind a curtain of shimmering blue silk.

"Throk," I whisper, tugging on his sleeve. "What's going on?"

He leans down, his breath warm against my ear. "Trust me. You're going to love this."

Before I can respond, Madam Whisper reappears, carrying a rolled-up carpet under her arm. It's smaller than I expected, maybe six feet long and four feet wide.

"Here we are," she says, laying it out on the floor. The carpet is a deep burgundy, intricately woven with gold thread in swirling patterns that seem to move when I look at them too long. "She's one of my best. Smooth ride, excellent handling, and a built-in heating charm for those chilly nights."

I blink, sure I've misheard. "I'm sorry, did you say 'ride?'"

Madam Whisper chuckles. "Oh yes, dear. This isn't just any carpet. It's a genuine flying carpet, straight from the looms of Agrabah."

I look from the carpet to Throk to Madam Whisper, waiting for someone to tell me this is all an elaborate joke, but they both just smile at me expectantly. "You can't be serious," I say weakly.

Throk kneels beside the carpet, running a hand over its surface. "Completely serious. Madam Whisper's carpets are the best in Evershift Haven. We use them for sky patrols and emergency rescues."

"Sky patrols," I repeat faintly. The room suddenly feels very warm.

Madam Whisper pats my arm sympathetically. "It's perfectly safe, dear. Throk here is an excellent pilot. You're in good hands."

I draw in a ragged breath, reminding myself I'm in a town where trees gossip and pumpkins come to life. Why not add flying carpets to the list?

"Okay," I say, squaring my shoulders. "Let's do this."

Throk beams at me before turning to Madam Whisper. "We'll have her back by midnight."

The old woman waves a hand dismissively. "Take your time, dears. The night is young, and love is in the air." She winks at me, and my cheeks grow hot.

Throk rolls out the carpet on the shop's small back porch. It hovers a few inches off the ground, rippling slightly as if caught in a breeze.

"Ladies first." He gestures grandly.

I eye the carpet warily before slowly lowering myself onto it. The fabric is surprisingly firm beneath me, almost like sitting on a very plush chair.

Throk settles in behind me, his broad chest warm against my back. "Hold on tightly," he murmurs, wrapping an arm around my waist.

Before I can ask what I'm supposed to hold onto, the carpet rises smoothly into the air. I let out a startled squeak, gripping his arm.

"It's okay," he says soothingly. "I've got you."

We glide forward, passing through an archway of wisteria that marks the edge of Madam Whisper's property, and then we're airborne, rising above the rooftops of Evershift Haven.

The town spreads out below us, a patchwork of twinkling lights and shadowy streets. The full moon hangs low in the sky, bathing everything in a soft, silvery glow.

"Oh," I say, my fear forgotten in the face of such beauty. "This is amazing."

He chuckles. "I told you you'd love it."

We soar higher, and it gets a little chilly until the heating charm kicks on. I gradually relax, leaning back against him. His arm tightens around me, and my stomach flutters for reasons that have nothing to do with our altitude.

"Look." He points with his free hand. "You can see the whole town from up here."

I look around, amazed by the view. The town square glows with festive lights while the Whispering Woods sway gently at the town's edge, leaves shimmering with an otherworldly light.

We drift lazily over the town as he points out landmarks and shares stories about each one. The Celestial Clock Tower chimes the hour, its gears visible through crystal-clear walls. A group of pixies dart past us, giggling and waving as they go.

"This place is incredible," I say, shaking my head in wonder. "I still can't believe it's real sometimes."

He's quiet for a moment. "What do you think about staying?" he asks softly. "I know I shouldn't ask you again already, but..."

I twist around to look at him, nearly losing my balance in the process. He steadies me, looking serious in the moonlight.

"You mean permanently?"

He nods. "I know it's a lot to ask. You have a life back in Chicago, but I've never met anyone like you. The way you've embraced Evershift Haven, how quickly you've adapted to all the magic and strangeness... This should be your home. With us." He pauses, swallowing hard. "With me."

I study his face, taking in the earnest expression along with the hope and vulnerability in his eyes. In the short time I've known him, Throk has shown me kindness, patience, and a world I never knew existed. I've been falling for him since the moment we met. "I think I'm falling in love with you."

His eyes widen as he beams. "Really?"

I nod, suddenly shy. "Really, but I have things to figure out. I'll let you know soon."

He looks disappointed but nods. "I won't push you again." He kisses me to make up for it, and there's nothing more magical than kissing an orc on a magic carpet ride.

Chapter 9

I WAKE TO THE SOUND of my phone vibrating on the nightstand. I guess I'm getting internet today. The way it comes and goes makes me suspect the town only lets messages through when it doesn't want to impress me in some other way—which sounds completely nuts but fits Evershift Haven.

Groggily, I reach for it, squinting at the bright screen. A text from Throk lights up the display:

"Your car's ready. Come by the shop when you can."

I blink, processing the information. It's only been a few days since I arrived in Evershift Haven. How did he fix it so quickly? Curiosity propels me out of bed. I throw on some clothes and head downstairs, nearly colliding with Crystal in the hallway.

"Good morning, Suzette," she says, her pale skin practically glowing in the dim light. "You're up early."

"Throk just texted. My car's fixed." I sound disappointed, and I am.

Crystal's eyebrows rise. "Already? That's unexpected."

I nod, sharing her surprise. "I'm heading over there now."

"Don't forget breakfast," Crystal calls after me as I hurry down the stairs.

The mid-October air is invigorating as I step outside. Evershift Haven seems quieter at this hour. I start walking, and as I approach the garage, I hear clanking tools and Throk's deep voice humming a tune I don't recognize. I knock on the open bay door.

His green head pops up from behind my car's open hood. His face breaks into a wide grin, tusks gleaming. "You're here early."

"Couldn't wait to see what magic you worked on my car," I say, walking closer.

He chuckles, wiping his hands on a rag. "A bit of both, actually. Mechanics and magic."

I peer into the engine compartment. Everything looks normal, but there's a faint shimmer in the air around certain components. Vivi still seems animated though, and she winks and grins at me. "What exactly did you do?"

Throk launches into an explanation, his enthusiasm infectious. "Well, the main issue was the magical interference from the town's barrier. It was disrupting your car's electrical systems. So, I installed a thaumic converter."

He points to a small, crystalline device nestled near the battery. "This little beauty harmonizes the magical energy with your car's technology. It should allow you to pass through the barrier without any problems now."

I stare at the device with awe and skepticism. "And it's safe?"

Throk nods confidently. "Absolutely. I've used this technique on several vehicles for out-of-towners. Works like a charm every time."

"That's incredible. So, I can leave whenever I want now?"

A flicker of disappointment crosses his face before he schools his expression. "That's right. You're free to go whenever you're ready."

The word 'free' reverberates in my mind. Am I ready to leave? The thought of returning to my normal life suddenly feels even less appealing than it did a few days ago.

Before I can respond, my phone starts ringing. I fish it out of my pocket, surprised to see my boss's name on the screen. I'd almost forgotten about work in the whirlwind of Evershift Haven, and I haven't worked on the Henderson case at all—mainly because it's not my case.

"I should take this," I say apologetically.

He nods understanding. "Go ahead. I'll finish up here and do a final check."

I step outside the garage and answer the call. "Hello?"

"Winters, where the hell are you?" Erik's voice blares through the speaker, making me wince.

"I'm still in Montana," I say, taken aback by his aggressive tone. "My car broke down, remember? I told you—"

"That was days ago. We have a major case coming up, and I need you in the office. Now."

A surge of anger rises. "I can't just teleport back to Chicago. My car—"

"I don't care about your car," he shouts. "Take a bus, rent a car, or whatever. Just get your ass back here."

The fury building inside me reaches a boiling point. How dare he speak to me like this? After all the late nights, the weekends sacrificed, and the personal life I've put on hold for this job? "You know what, Erik? I quit."

There's a moment of stunned silence on the other end. "What did you say?"

"I said, I quit," I repeat, louder this time. "I'm done with the unreasonable demands, the lack of respect, all of it. Find someone else to be your legal workhorse."

"You can't just—" He starts, but I cut him off.

"I can, and I am. Goodbye, Erik. Don't bother calling again."

I end the call and exhale sharply as ebbing adrenaline leaves me sagging. Did I really just do that?

I turn back to the garage and find Throk standing in the doorway, looking concerned. "Everything okay? You were shouting."

I let out a shaky laugh. "I just quit my job."

Throk blinks. "Wow. That's...big. How do you feel?"

I pause, taking stock of my emotions. There's fear and uncertainty, yes, but mostly relief. Excitement, even. "Surprisingly good. I should have done it a long time ago."

I look up at Throk with myriad emotions swirling inside me. I've just quit my job and decided to stay in this magical town, and that hits me all at once. It's terrifying and exhilarating at the same time. "I want to stay here in Evershift Haven. With you."

A smile spreads across his face. "Really? You mean it?"

I nod, feeling more certain with each passing second. "I do. I don't know exactly what I'll do here yet, but I want to figure it out, and I want to do it with you by my side."

His hand envelops mine. "Nothing would make me happier."

He pulls me close, and I lean into his broad chest. I tilt my head up, and our lips meet in a passionate kiss. It's different from our previous kisses—this one feels like a promise and a beginning.

When we finally part, both slightly breathless, he grins down at me. "If you're staying, we should probably figure out your living situation."

I laugh. "Good point. I don't think Crystal and Etienne want me as a permanent guest at the 'Moonlit Inn.'"

There's a hint of nervousness in his voice when he says, "You could stay with me until we find a bigger place to share."

It's fast, maybe too fast, but something about it feels right. "Are you sure? I don't want to impose."

Throk shakes his head, his long black hair swaying with the movement. "You wouldn't be imposing at all. I want you there."

I smile up at him. "Yes, I'd love to stay with you."

He lets out a whoop of joy that startles a nearby flock of enchanted pigeons, sending them fluttering into the air in a shower of sparkles. I giggle at his enthusiasm.

"We should celebrate. How about a tour of Evershift Haven in your newly repaired car? I'm sure Vivi is eager to explore its new magical home."

As if on cue, my car's headlights flash, and its engine purrs to life. I jump slightly, still not used to its semi-sentient nature.

"I think that's a yes," I say, grinning at Throk.

We climb into the car, Throk folding his large frame into the passenger seat with surprising grace. As soon as we're settled, the car starts moving on its own, pulling out of the garage and onto the street.

"Whoa." I grip the steering wheel even though I'm not controlling it. "Is this normal?"

Throk chuckles. "For a magical car in Evershift Haven? Absolutely. Just relax and enjoy the ride. Your car knows where it wants to go."

I force myself to loosen my grip on the wheel, absorbing the strange sensation of being driven by my own vehicle. We cruise down the main street, passing by now-familiar sights like "The Enchanted Espresso" and "Spellbound Cinema."

Approaching the town square, I gasp in amazement. The entire area has transformed since I last saw it. The trees are now adorned with twinkling fairy lights, and colorful banners announcing the "Evershift Haven Welcome Festival" flutter in the breeze.

"What's all this?" I ask, gesturing at the festive decorations.

Throk's eyes twinkle with mischief. "Oh, just a little something the town whipped up to welcome its newest resident."

My jaw drops. "You mean...me?"

He nods, grinning widely. "Word travels fast in a magical town. Especially when the trees are such terrible gossips." He grins. "The Halloween and autumnal decor will return after today."

Before I can respond, my car pulls to a stop in front of the Heart of Haven, the ancient oak tree at the center of the square. As soon as we step out, we're greeted by a chorus of cheers and applause.

It seems like the entire town has gathered to welcome me. Mayor Ambrosius Windless steps forward, his long white beard nearly touching the ground. He clears his throat and speaks in a voice that carries across the square without the need for amplification. "Citizens of Evershift Haven, we're gathered here today to welcome our newest resident, Suzette Winters."

Another round of cheers erupts, I flush with embarrassment and pleasure.

The mayor turns to address me directly. "In choosing to make Evershift Haven your home, you have also chosen to become part of our magical community. We welcome you with open arms and open hearts."

He gestures to a nearby table, where a large scroll of parchment unfurls itself. "If you would be so kind as to sign our town register, you will officially become a citizen of Evershift Haven."

I approach the table, feeling a bit dazed by the whole experience. A quill floats up to meet my hand.

"Just sign on the dotted line, dearie. The ink's enchanted to never fade."

With a deep breath and a thorough read—I'm still an attorney—I take the quill and sign my name on the parchment. As soon as I finish the last letter, the ink glows golden for a moment before settling into the page.

Mayor Windless claps his hands together. "Excellent. Let the Welcome Festival begin."

The square erupts into activity. Music starts playing from nowhere and everywhere at once, a lively tune that makes me want to dance. Food stalls appear as if by magic (which, I remind myself, it probably is), offering an array of delectable treats.

Throk takes my hand, beaming with pride. "How does it feel to be an official resident of Evershift Haven?"

I squeeze his hand, still trying to process everything. "It feels... right. Like I've finally found where I belong."

He pulls me close and kisses me softly. "I'm so glad you're staying," he murmurs against my lips.

We kiss once again, and the Heart of Haven behind us seems to glow a little brighter, its leaves rustling in a nonexistent breeze. I've made the right choice. Evershift Haven is my home now, and I'm in the arms of the man—orc—that I love.

A COUPLE OF DAYS LATER, I sit on the edge of my bed in Throk's cozy apartment, talking to my sister. Candice has already received the news I'm staying in Evershift Haven. She had a mini freakout but seems to have calmed down now.

As I talk, I hear the front door open and close. Heavy footsteps approach the bedroom, and Throk appears in the doorway. He smiles when he sees me, his tusks glinting in the soft light of the bedside lamp.

I hold up a finger, mouthing "My sister" to him. He nods in understanding and moves to sit beside me on the bed, the mattress dipping under his weight.

"...and then he asked me to stay," I finish, wrapping up my sanitized version of events. "And I realized I wanted to, and I want you to come meet him for Thanksgiving."

"That's so romantic." She sighs again. "I can't wait to meet him. He sounds perfect for you, Suz."

I roll against Throk, who wraps an arm around my shoulders. "He really is," I say softly.

"Okay, I should let you go," Candice says. "I've got a lot to plan if I'm coming for Thanksgiving. Text me the details, okay?"

"Will do," I say. "Love you, Candi."

"Love you too, Suz, and I'm happy for you, really. Even if I think you're a little crazy."

I laugh. "Thanks. See you soon."

As I end the call, Throk raises an eyebrow. "So, how did it go?"

I let out a long breath. "Better than I expected, actually. She's coming for Thanksgiving."

Throk blinks. "That's great. But...how are we going to explain, well, everything?"

I chew on my lower lip, considering the challenge ahead. "I don't know. I didn't tell her about the magic. I figured it would be better for her to see it for herself."

Throk nods slowly. "Probably a wise choice. It's not exactly something you can explain over the phone."

"No kidding," I snort. "Can you imagine? 'Hey, sis, by the way, I'm living in a magical town full of supernatural creatures. My new boyfriend? Oh, he's an orc. No big deal.'"

Throk chuckles, the sound rumbling through his chest. "When you put it that way, it does sound a bit ridiculous."

I turn to face him, suddenly serious. "Throk, what if she can't handle it? What if she thinks I've lost my mind?"

He cups my face in his large hands, his touch gentle despite his strength. "Then we'll deal with it together. Your sister loves you. She might be shocked at first, but I'm sure she'll come around."

I press against his touch, drawing comfort from his presence. "I hope you're right."

"Of course I am," he says with a grin. "I'm always right about these things. It's an orc thing."

I laugh, some of my tension easing. "Oh really? An orc thing, huh?"

"Absolutely." He nods solemnly. "We're known for our wisdom and insight into human family dynamics."

I playfully swat his arm. "You're ridiculous."

"Maybe, but I made you laugh."

I smile up at him. "That you did. Thank you." I kiss him and say, "Thanks for everything, my love." I can't wait to show Candice the town, but for now, my orc lover is busy stripping me, and I have to address that priority.

About Aurelia

AURELIA SKYE IS THE pen name *USA Today* bestselling author Kit Tunstall uses when writing science fiction and paranormal romance, along with paranormal women's fiction. It's simply a way to separate the myriad types of stories she writes so readers know what to expect with each "author."

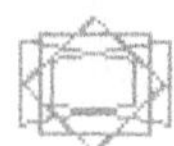

Also by Aurelia Skye

Alien Baby Pact
Baby For The Brundle Commander
Baby For The Serp General
Alien Baby Pact Compilation
Baby For The Grimlock General
Baby For The Palantir Chief
Baby For The Alphan Captain
Baby For The Mosaic Med Chief
Baby For The Tark Commander

Alien Baby Pakt
Alien Baby Pakt Zusammenstellung

BioCircuit Nexus
Cyborgs' Origins
Cyborg's Tether

Celestial Mates
Wrong Place, Right Mate
Destined For The Drakari Warlords

Cybernetic Hearts
Mated To The Cyborg General
Claimed By The Cyborg Commander
Fated For The Cyborg Officer
Meant For The Cyborg Captain
Baby For The Cyborg General
Cybernetic Hearts: Complete Series
Cœurs Cybernétiques: Série Complète

Dazon Agenda
Written In The Stars
Alien's Babies
Diplomatic Affairs
Moon Madness
Across The Stars
Emperor's Assassin Bride
Dazon Agenda: Complete Collection
Compilation de l'Agenda Dazon

Evershift Haven
Pumpkin Spice and Orc's Delight

Future Fairytales
Hooked

Guerriers Blessés
Chassé

Séancen Und Schlaffe Haut
Nekromantie Und Knieschmerzen
Marids und Gedächtnisverlust
Teufelsgeschäfte Und Schwindelzauber
Happy Ends Und Neuanfängen
Höllenhunde & Mistelzweige

Hell Virus
Catching Hell
Surviving Hell
Bleeding Hell
Raising Hell
Sharing Hell

Howls Romance
The Jaguar Alpha's Forbidden Lover
CEO Wolf Shifter's Surprise Twins

Northstar Shifters
Northstar Heir's Scarred Mate

Olympus Station
Station Commander's Surrogate
Alien Prince's Secret Baby
Security Agent's Alien Bartender
Olympus Station Compilation

SpicyShorts
Music In My Heart
Kilted Tentacle Monster: A Search for True Love

Sweet Escapes
Hook & Wendy

The Haunting of Clara Gray
Ghostly Awakening
Ghostly Harmonies

Three Crones Inn
Vastly Inn-proved
Ghastly Intentions
Grave Inn-tervention
Ghostly Inn-heritance
Three Crones Inn Compilation

True North
True North #1: Death & Deception
True North #2: Rescued & Revelations
True North #3: Fire & Ice
True North #4: Enemies & Lovers
True North #5: Truth & Tiranog
True North #6: Fight & Flight
True North #7: Love & Loss

Wounded Warriors
Relentless
Marked
Justice
Wounded Warriors Collection
Hunted

Standalone
Reluctant Companion
Princess By Mistake
Fire Lord's Assistant
True North
Dragon Laird's Witch
Alien General's Rebel Consort
Tempted By Demons
Enemy Combatant
Grotesquerie
Mistaken Bounty
Wahre Richtung
Power Surges & Amorous Urges
Taken By The Orc General
Compilation Alien Baby Pact